STERLING NORTH was born in a farmhouse on the shore of Lake Koshkonong in Wisconsin and was raised in the nearby town of Edgerton. After attending the University of Chicago he became a newspaper reporter and later was Literary Editor of several newspapers. He has written dozens of articles and poetry for most major American magazines, and is the author of twenty-nine books, which have been published on five continents and in more than fifty languages. These include the bestselling RASCAL and RACCOONS ARE THE BRIGHTEST PEOPLE, which also appear in this series, and THE WOLFLING.

He and his wife, Gladys, live on twenty-seven acres near Morristown, New Jersey, where their neighbors include foxes, deer, and, of course, raccoons.

The cover art is by Brad Holland.

SO DEAR
TO MY HEART

Sterling North

 CAMELOT BOOKS/PUBLISHED BY AVON

AVON BOOKS
A division of
The Hearst Corporation
959 Eighth Avenue
New York, New York 10019

First Camelot Printing, (Third Printing), October, 1965

Fourth Printing, November, 1969

CAMELOT TRADEMARK REG. U.S. PAT. OFF. AND
FOREIGN COUNTRIES, REGISTERED TRADEMARK—
MARCA REGISTRADA, HECHO EN CHICAGO, U.S.A.

Printed in Canada

CONTENTS

1 SPRING COMES TO CAT HOLLOW

The bull calf had been sold. Jeremiah's desperate prayer had not been answered. He was as empty as a dry gourd; as lonely as a solitary whippoorwill in the night. In the cool of the morning he went alone into the garden on the hill to the east of the cabin to spade the brown earth where the pole beans and sweet corn would soon be planted.

Granny Kincaid, who said that sloth was sin and that the Lord God sent man forth from the Garden of Eden to till the ground, watched with a heavy heart as Jeremiah climbed the hill against the April sky. The boy was like his grandfather David Kincaid who had died when the spice bush was in bloom thirteen years ago that spring. Both had the Kincaid fire and sweetness; stiff-starch proud, ready to argue with Granny or with the Lord God Almighty; quick to forgive on small matters, but running as deep as Blue Lick River on problems of importance.

As he drove the spade into the earth and lifted with

all his strength the heavy clods, Jeremiah was thinking that Granny Kincaid had laid down more commandments than Jehovah; not even the Bible could name so many vanities nor things of the flesh. The dull ache in his heart for the loss of his bull calf was not soothed by the first white fire along the blossom boughs or the upsurge of new green. He saw the bright sunlight as through a smoked glass, and only dimly felt the tremendous rush of spring which had come pouring like a tide up the Mississippi and Ohio valleys, flooding such tributaries as Blue Lick River and Bean Blossom Creek all the way to the very source of the mint-cool water in the Kincaid springhouse.

Thou shalt not trespass upon the Tarleton land. Thou shalt not question thy own beginnings. Thou shalt not run away to Fulton Corners. Thou shalt not weep for thy slaughtered bull calf. Thou shalt honor thy granny who hath made all these commandments.

Strange, Jeremiah thought, that this same Granny Kincaid could also play gay ballad songs on her dulcimer, could bake mouth-watering Scripture cake, could weave the most beautiful kivers in Pike County, could dance every square dance known to the hills, could doctor him tenderly with herbs and poultices when he was ailing.

But on this April morning in the spring of 1903, as Jeremiah spaded the garden on the hill overlooking their weather-beaten cabin in southern Indiana, the thought of Granny was gall and wormwood in his mouth. Blueberry's long-legged bull calf had eyes as big as brown walnuts. His silky hide was velvet-smooth. He was always hungry, always eager to suck Jeremiah's fingers. Probably at this moment Mr. Turner was whetting his sharp, cherry-handled butcher knife; was fastening the struggling little bull to the iron hooks, pulling the rope that lifted him bawling wildly into the terrifying place of death above the blood trough.

Granny had done that. Granny had sold his bull calf to Mr. Turner. Jeremiah hated Granny Kincaid; he would never forgive her. Maybe he would hook a ride on the tender of Old 99, when it came through;

8

he would go far outland to some distant town like Midlothian where no one had ever heard of Granny and Granny would never again hear of him. On Old 99, with its lonesome whistle and wonderful bell, he would go swirling and whooshing away into a distant world where there were no commandments and where a boy could keep his beloved bull calf.

It was a good thing he had brought three or four apples in his shirt. He might get hungry on his long journey. Maybe outland somewhere he could find where his pap and mam were buried in their distant bury holes. He would put fresh spring flowers on their graves —laurel blossoms or pink dogwood or redbud.

Jeremiah threw down his spade and lay in the warm grass under the new-feathered, lacy shade of the mulberry tree where a redbird was whistling "What-cheer! What-cheer!" He thought of his room under the eaves, and the sound of Granny racking her loom in the great room below. He thought of the cool, dank cellar full of hams and bacons and preserves. He knew he was lying to himself about running away. And suddenly he remembered that thinking of doing an evil thing is as wicked as doing it.

So he asked God to forgive him for hating Granny and wanting to run away. But he was still miserable and lonesome.

He began to take off his copper-tipped shoes and his long black stockings. He would go barefoot without so much as a by-your-leave and he would run away at least as far as Fulton Corners to see Uncle Hiram and Tildy. He didn't care if he caught his death of cold because it would serve Granny right for selling his bull calf.

An outlander might have called Fulton Corners a jerkwater or a whistle stop. But to Jeremiah it was a place of high adventure. You could sit on a pile of railroad ties under the mossy water tank and wait for the great moment when Old 99 came around the distant bend. Or you could press your nose against the sooty window of the station and watch Bob Peters click-clacking messages over the mysterious telegraph wires. Or you could sit in Al's barbershop and listen to old Grandpa Meeker tell how he saved Fulton Corners singlehanded from the Confederacy when Morgan's Raiders came thundering into town during the Civil War.

There was a big grain elevator where a man was once smothered in ten thousand bushels of wheat, and a little church with a ladder to the belfry, and a haunted graveyard filled with sad white marble stones topped by doves or clasped hands or sometimes a lamb if the corpse had been a baby. Fud Grundy said there were dim lights and wailing haunts in that graveyard on stormy nights, but Fud was the biggest liar in Fulton Township. Maybe that was because Fud's father owned the store. Jerry didn't care if Granny and the Lord God Almighty both said "Thou shalt not covet." He coveted like anything the stag-handled jackknife with four blades and a corkscrew and a bottle opener in Grundy's mercantile store. There was a true-tempered hand ax with a red handle that could make any boy covetous, glass marbles with more colors than the rainbow, red-and-green fishing bobbers, and twenty kinds of candy. Jeremiah thought that Heaven must be something like Pete Grundy's general store. Thinking about all the plunder in that wonderful emporium almost helped him to forget his brown-eyed bull calf who must be dead and skinned by now and all cut up into veal.

Jeremiah sighed deeply and started across the dusty street toward Hiram Douglas's blacksmith shop. He had an idea. If Uncle Hiram had Granny's cultivator ready, maybe she would forgive him for running away to Fulton Corners. Hiram was singing "Sourwood Mountain" as Jerry approached the shop:

> *"Chickens acrowin' on Sourwood Mountain,*
> *Hay did-dy ump did-dy id-dy um day,*
> *So many pretty girls I can't count 'em,*
> *Hay did-dy ump did-dy id-dy um day."*

10

Like the Kincaids and the Tarletons, Hiram Douglas had come north into Indiana from the Cumberland region of Kentucky. He had the skills of the Scotch-Irish mountaineers and could make hundreds of useful objects from wood or metal. He could split hand-riven shakes for a roof that would turn the rain for fifty years. He could weave white-oak withes into the lastingest seat that ever pleasured a weary bottom seeking the comfort of a hickory settin' chair. He could whittle a whistle from slippery elm; carve a hound dog true as Scripture chasing a ring-tailed, sassy coon. And he could make a dulcimer to charm the Seraphim and Cherubim.

Uncle Hiram had been a hell-raiser in his day, and he still had pictures of Anna Held and Lillian Russell tacked up beside his portraits of Dan Patch and other prominent race horses. But in recent years he had been tapering off on applejack, insisting that corn liquor and Methodist hymns made too potent a blend in the choir loft on Sunday.

For a burly blacksmith who shod most of the horses of Fulton Township, Uncle Hiram had surprisingly sensitive fingers, plucking chords on his guitar while he sang "Sourwood Mountain":

> *"My true love is a sunburnt daisy.*
> *She won't work and I'm too lazy . . ."*

His rich applejack baritone voice floated out of the shop as Jeremiah scuffed his bare feet through the flour-fine dust toward the wide front door. Yes, there sat Uncle Hiram, blue-eyed, sandy-haired, sprawling on the luxurious settee he had made from an old surrey seat and two sets of springs singing:

> *"The big dogs bark and the little dogs bite you,*
> *Hay did-dy ump did-dy id-dy um day.*
> *The big girls spark and the little girls fight you,*
> *Hay did-dy ump did-dy id-dy um day."*

When Uncle Hiram saw Jeremiah crossing the road

11

he laid aside his guitar, and although he continued to sing "Sourwood Mountain" his fingers took up another task. He was finishing a whipstock-lash hand-grip on a fifteen-foot Calcutta bamboo fish pole. Just now he was completing the intricate turn and fancy braiding at the very butt of the pole.

"Good morning, Uncle Hiram."

"Good morning, Jeremiah."

Yes, Hiram Douglas thought, I can see by his face that Granny sold the little bull. He's aching to ask about this fish pole, but Granny's taught him not to hint. He's run away again and he figures if I'll fix the cultivator, he'll have an alibi for visiting the Corners. Looks as though I got started on this Calcutta just in the nick of time.

"Now this pole," said Uncle Hiram slowly, "is purely a delight. Right length, right heft, right snap, and everything."

"It's real handsome," Jeremiah said, trying not to let his hunger for the beautiful rod creep into his voice.

"Purtiest piece of bamboo I ever laid eyes on." His fingers worked swiftly on the intricate pattern. "It's going to pleasure me next time I go fishing."

"You mean," asked Jeremiah with anguish barely concealed, "you're afixin' it for your ownself?" He could have bitten his tongue for being so forward. It was brash and ill-mannered to let Hiram see his heartbreak.

"Well, I ain't afixin' it for Fud Grundy."

"Fud don't need it," Jeremiah said sadly. "His pap's got a whole rack of store-bought tackle."

"Long, strong, and full of give," said Uncle Hiram, stealing a glance at the woebegone Jeremiah. "Hook a bluegill quicker than lightning; stout enough to hold the Big One."

"He's under the covered bridge," Jeremiah whispered. "I seen him this morning. He's the whoppin'est silver catfish in Blue Lick River. I'm agoin' to catch him iffen it takes me the rest of my natural-born days."

"Got me some braided line and some number-10 hooks," Uncle Hiram said. "Got me the purtiest red-

12

and-green bobber ever floated on water. Gonna put a wad of night crawlers as big as your fist on that there hook and . . ."

Jeremiah swallowed hard and blinked his eyes so Hiram wouldn't notice how trembly he was deep down inside. Maybe someday he could earn enough money to buy a Calcutta bamboo for his ownself, all golden and shining and purty as sunup. Maybe Uncle Hiram would teach him the whipstock braid so he could fashion such a beautiful grip to fit the hand.

"You got a job of work I could do?" Jeremiah asked.

"What you want a job of work for, son?"

"Earn me some cash money."

"What you want cash money for, Jerry?"

"Buy me a Calcutta pole and some braided line like yourn," Jeremiah said.

"That's a real good idea," Uncle Hiram admitted, picking up the broken cultivator shovel from Granny's cultivator and crossing to the forge. "Now you put your back into pumping the bellows, blow up a real good fire, and we'll see how long it takes."

"To fix the cultivator?"

"To earn that Calcutta fish pole," Uncle Hiram said, grinning down at the boy whose eyes were now shining with joy and disbelief. Jeremiah knew he should say "thank you kindly," but for the moment he didn't dare trust himself to speak. The fire roared; the hammer on the anvil was like a church bell pealing tidings. The hiss of hot metal in the mossy oak tub was purely joyous. Out of sheer exuberance he reached up to catch a flying spark.

"Careful, Jeremiah. Them ain't lightning bugs."

A farmer came in with a team of Percherons to be shod. So after Jerry had served his turn at the bellows he took Uncle Hiram's Sears, Roebuck catalogue and curled up on the surrey seat. Usually he coveted hundreds of items in the "dream book." But today he was so plumb contented he could enjoy every page without so much as a wistful sigh. It was a wonder·and a revelation to see this other world of scrollwork furni-

13

ture, buggies with bright red wheels, nobby new shoes, and classy watch fobs.

Autoharps, zith-o-harps, mandolins, and parlor organs vied with corsets, cuckoo clocks, wigs, and windmills. And if you bought Dr. King's new discovery for consumption, coughs, and colds, or Dr. Hostetter's remarkable alcoholic bitters and neither one could save your life, you could always be buried in Sears's best plush-lined coffin (please state size) to go with Sears's unchallengeable tombstones of marble or Vermont granite. Sears sold it and Old 99 delivered it, from rubber nipples and teething rings through bridal gowns to permanent wreaths of suitably mournful metal flowers. You lived the whole cycle from birth to death reading the Sears, Roebuck dream book.

Jeremiah hadn't heard Mathilda Wheaton come into the blacksmith shop until she was beside him looking over his shoulder at the catalogue. Jerry took Tildy for granted. She came out to Cat Hollow to go hickory nutting sometimes. Often they fished together at the covered bridge. And they had a secret place in a ravine where Tildy pretended she could see little people. She reached into Jerry's shirt to get an apple and munched it happily.

"Notice anything different about me?"

"You look same as always," Jerry said.

"Maw made me this new dress; it's purty."

Uncle Hiram had finished his horseshoeing so he picked up his guitar and began to play a dance tune.

"Remember how I showed you, Tildy?"

She remembered. And while the big man played and sang she bowed and pirouetted, sashayed and cut neat pigeonwings. Uncle Hiram complimented Tildy on her new dress.

"Makes mighty purty dresses, your maw does."

Tildy grinned happily, never missing a step in her dance. She had hoped he would notice. But now she remembered her other purpose in coming: a message from her mother, the village dressmaker.

"Oh—and Mamma said the belt's getting looser and

14

the treadle's slipping worse, and you've got to fix her sewing machine like you promised."

Uncle Hiram yawned, stretched, and put aside his guitar.

"You tell your maw she should read the third chapter of Ecclesiastes," he said. " 'To every thing there is a season. . . a time to be born, and a time to die . . . a time to weep and a time to laugh; a time to mourn, and a time to dance.' "

The boy and the girl waited patiently, knowing that Uncle Hiram took his time reaching the point of a story. It was pleasanter that way.

"A time to fix sewing machines and a time to fix cultivators," the big man said, yawning enormously. "I'm agettin' around to it, but the work's piling up."

Hiram also reached into Jerry's shirt for an apple.

Far away, clear-toned and sorrowful, the train whistle sounded, the echoes ricocheting through the hills.

Hiram pulled his silver stem-winder from his pocket. "Right on time," he said.

It would be another full minute before Old 99 nosed proudly around the bend, big with the knowledge of great cities like Evansville and Indianapolis at either end of its portentous run. The rails began to sing with secret anticipation. The distant river bridge roared its hollow welcome.

"Reckon she'll stop?" Jeremiah asked hopefully. There was always the off-chance that Highball Johnson, the engineer, would go streaking through town like a specter hound at cock's crow, scornfully tossing the mailbag to the station platform, leaving the Corner hurt and embarrassed and smoldering with vague resentment.

"I reckon," Uncle Hiram said, wishing it so, if only for the sake of these two children peering up the track.

Screen doors slammed. The Corners stirred from its drowsy lethargy and came to life. Colts in their green pastures went frisking on long, slender legs as though a windstorm were brewing. From dreams of mortal battles with ring-tailed varmints fiery-eyed in lantern light, old coon dogs ceased to twitch and whine in their sleep, opened heavy-lidded eyes, and trotted for the station. Chickens, clucking irritably, left their cool dust baths underneath the bridalwreath Spiraea. The checker game broke up in Grundy's store.

"Hey, Paw! She's ablowin' for a stop," Fud Grundy shouted.

Yes, traintime was ever the best moment of the day in Fulton Corners, for the papers and the Civil War pensions, the infrequent letters and the even more infrequent visitors came on the train. It was a social gathering that broke the monotony of the morning, with Storekeeper Grundy handing out the mail and playing ill-mannered host. Bob Peters, still wearing his limp and his campaign hat from the Spanish-American War, was well aware of his importance as stationmaster.

"Stand back, folks. Don't crowd now."

The mere fact that the train was stopping satisfied Jeremiah. Then his eye caught the additional wonder which was to make this a banner day in his memory.

It must be purely sinful, Jeremiah thought, to be so joyous as he now was over the strange sight which greeted his eyes. Granny, who hated trains and race horses and the fleshpots of Egypt in general, would never have approved the warm glow in the pit of his stomach, the tingling at the roots of his hair, and the ice water along his spine.

There, at the end of the old-fashioned combination train, there, all brightly varnished in golden yellow like his new Calcutta pole, was a private railroad car. Intricate scrolls of purple and magenta, volutes of mauve and silver beautified the whole. And across the car in scarlet letters ran the legend: "Dan Patch, Champion of Champions." Was he dreaming? Framed beneath the windows from which the world's most famous race horse viewed the hills of Indiana was a full-color portrait of the great racing stallion.

"I'd ruther see Dan Patch than the President of the whole United States," Jeremiah said.

A murmur ran through the awed assembly. "Dan Patch!" "Fastest horse in creation!" "Reckon he's in there?" "Never thought I'd live to see the day."

As though in answer to their questions the center

16

doors of the shining car rolled back, a cleated ramp was lowered like a drawbridge. From the darkly gleaming interior of paneled wood and polished brasswork stepped a bantam-rooster-of-a-man with a brick-red face, green derby hat, and violet waistcoat. A heavy gold chain across his ample paunch ended in a horseshoe good-luck charm.

"Stand back, folks," the trainer shouted in a voice made guttural by the dust of many tracks, allayed by the moisture of many a bottle.

"Stand back," Bob Peters echoed.

"Stand back, little girl, you want to get hurt?" the trainer said to Tildy. Jerry too was crowding close.

"You heard what he said! Stand back!" Fud Grundy gave Jeremiah a vigorous shove.

Down the ramp came two grooms leading the sleek brown stallion in a blue, crimson, and gold blanket. The monogram "D.P." appliquéd in silk on either flank proved, if further proof were needed, that this was indeed Dan Patch.

Uncle Hiram had told Jeremiah enough about Prince Alert, and the brilliant little chestnut mare, Lou Dillon, and the great-hearted stallion Dan Patch so that the boy felt he really knew the trotters and pacers whose pictures were tacked to the walls of the blacksmith shop. He knew that the pacer now coming down the ramp was supposed to be too short of body and too heavy through the shoulders to be really handsome. But those were minute imperfections spoken of lovingly by a doting nation.

"Fastest thing on four legs," the trainer boasted, "but gentle as a lamb. Steady roadster. Any child can drive him."

"Reckon that critter can pace the mile in two minutes?" a farmer asked.

"He'll hit one fifty-five one of these days," the trainer said confidently.

"Seems kinda peculiar," Pete Grundy belittled; "fastest thing on four legs and you're scairt to race him."

"Ain't nothing in his class to put him up against," the

17

trainer said. "See that grin on Dan Patch's face? He knows when he hears a dam-fool remark."

Hiram chuckled. Most of the crowd laughed uneasily. Too many of them owed money to the storekeeper to show their pleasure. Grundy subsided, scowling, a trifle jealous of the horse who had stolen his role at traintime. The grooms removed the emblazoned blanket, snapped a plunge line to the stallion's halter, and let him exercise in a fifty-foot circle. The ankles swathed in white wool flashed in the sun. The precise feet with their polished hoofs moved like clockwork. The silky muscles rippled in an effortless flow of tremendous power. Even the storekeeper forgot himself in the spectacle.

"Now what?" asked Grandpa Meeker, as a gigantic Negro swipe came down the ramp carrying a brass-bound cedar tub. He was followed by a second Negro of equal size carrying a ten-gallon milk can on his shoulder.

"Must be his drinking water," Bob Peters decided.

"Jehoshaphat," said Grandpa, spitting a long stream of tobacco juice. "I raised ten young'uns on creek water."

As the stallion drank deeply from the tub, the trainer lifted each hoof to examine it carefully. "There's a loose nail in this shoe, Abe."

"Pawed it loose, Mr. Burns," the swipe said. "He gets real restless cooped up in that car."

"He'll throw that shoe before we reach Louisville," the trainer prophesied. "One of you men a blacksmith?"

Hiram stepped forward, picked up the stallion's foot and held it between his knees. "Nail's bent," he said. "I'll put in a new one."

"Hammer and pincers, Abe," the trainer shouted.

"Yes, suh."

As the swipe disappeared into the car, the horse raised his great dewy muzzle, widened his nostrils, and snuffed the air delicately. Jeremiah was so close he could have touched the heavily muscled shoulders with his hand. The stallion turned toward him with what seemed a friendly grin, the big ears went up sharply,

18

and the wide-spaced eyes gleamed with mischief as he reached for the boy's apple. Humorous self-assurance born of long pampering (swipes who crooned to him and an owner who idolized him) had made the big pacer almost human in his eccentricities. Jerry trembled with excitement as the stallion nuzzled at his sleeve.

"He wants your apple, son," the trainer said.

"Can I . . . ?" Jerry began. He wanted to say there was nothing in the world he would rather do than feed Dan Patch his apple. But the cat got his tongue.

"Ain't wormy, is it?" The trainer examined the apple and returned it.

"Oh, no, sir."

"All right. You can give it to him."

Breathlessly, his face shining with pleasure, Jeremiah held out the apple on the flattened palm of his trembling hand. The stallion took it delicately like a gentleman, his velvet muzzle just touching Jerry, sending a chill of pleasant excitement along his outstretched arm. The big teeth crunched, while the boy watched with rapt wonder and admiration.

"He can have mine too," Tildy offered.

"Sorry, young lady," the trainer grinned. "One's enough. Have to be careful with champions. Don't want him to get the colic."

The swipe had returned with hammer and pincers. Hiram reached into the pocket of his leather apron for a nail. It was a work of seconds to pull the loose nail, drive home the new one and clinch it. The big stallion was gentle and fearless as Hiram worked on his well-groomed hoof. Instinctively man and horse trusted each other.

Hiram carefully retrieved the old nail from the ground, stood erect, and handed the swipe the tools. Jerry's eyes followed every move.

"What do I owe you?" the trainer asked, reaching for his wallet.

"I'll just keep this nail."

"All right, boys, we'd better get rolling."

Two seconds later the amiable keeper and trainer

of the champion had Fud Grundy by the ear. "Leave that mane alone," he shouted.

Fud broke away and ran, trying to hide his jackknife as he slipped to the back of the crowd.

"They'd shave every hair of his tail and mane if we let 'em," the trainer fumed. "Folks steal his shoes, his blankets, and even oats out of his manger. . . . Well, get aboard, boys."

Up the ramp went the men and the horse. The doors of the shining private car rolled shut. Highball Johnson rang the bell of Old 99, blew the whistle, and waved lazily at the folks of Fulton Corners. Slowly he advanced the throttle, steam hissed into the cylinders, and Dan Patch was gone forever from their lives. Never again would Jeremiah see the fabulous pacer. But all his life he would remember the touch of his muzzle on his hand and the sheen of his rich coat shining in the sun on that April morning. And he would wear all his life the ring that Uncle Hiram made for him from that loose nail in the shoe of Dan Patch.

Although Granny Kincaid held that horse racing and card playing were the devil's pastimes, she could quote the Scriptures to prove that fishing was an occupation approved by the Lord. Hadn't Jesus, walking by the Sea of Galilee, come upon two brothers, Simon called Peter and Andrew his brother casting a net into the sea? And did He not say to them, "I will make you fishers of men"? What was good enough for the Lord's disciples was good enough for a Kincaid. Besides, the thought of fresh-caught catfish fried a golden brown made Granny as hungry as a she-wolf with whelps.

"If you're cravin' mouth-waterin' victuals," Granny would often say, "you can't beat catfish and johnny-cake."

So Jeremiah, feeling sharp as a fox in a chicken coop, had it all figured out. He would not only lure Uncle Hiram into delivering the repaired cultivator, but they would stop at the covered bridge and try the new pole on those fighting fork-tailed silver cats

20

lying in the deep hole below the riffles. Granny couldn't be angry if he brought home both cultivator and catfish.

Broad-beamed Uncle Hiram nearly filled the seat of his one-horse jolt wagon. So Jeremiah and Tildy had to stand behind the seat, legs wide apart, to take the lurching. Talk about the rocky road to Dublin! It was the King's highway compared to the Devil's wash board from Fulton Corners to Cat Hollow. The creaking wheels thumped over the limestone ledges with violence. It made the young'uns laugh until Uncle Hiram wondered if they were "teched in the haid." The children's laughter and the soft air of the April afternoon put Hiram in a ballad-singing mood, so he began to make up a song as they jolted along:

> *"Come on, plug, get offen that dime;*
> *Bag of Bones cain't make no time—*
> *Hiram's hoss ain't no Dan Patch,*
> *Turtle could whop him in a pacin' match."*

The spine-jolting ride furnished unexpected syncopation as the trio joined their voices in variations on "Old Dan Tucker," celebrating the horse they had seen, the new fish pole they were about to try, and the sheer joy of being alive.

The road smoothed out as they approached the bridge. Newly-green willows brushed them gently. Jeremiah's heart was in his mouth as the river came into view. His hunger to get his line into the water was like a sweet agony. His nostrils tingled with the smell of mint and wet earth and running water. Redwing blackbirds flooded the willow grove with their liquid notes; black terns wheeled and cried in stormy discord over the water while a bullfrog played the bottom note on the bass fiddle in a reedy bayou.

Fishing was a kind of madness with Jeremiah; and everything that went with it partook of a soaring wild music of sight and sound and touch and odor—the belted kingfisher plummeting from his lookout, the rush of white water subsiding into slowly whirling pools

21

of secret depth, the tang of flag roots and peat, the springy soil beneath his bare feet.

It was a matter of moments to break clods from the moist bank and find a generous baiting of worms. Another moment and he had skillfully tossed his hook below the riffle into the dark and promising hole where the Big One lay.

Only then did he remember that he had not offered Uncle Hiram or Tildy first chance with the pole. But he had no opportunity to apologize, for the buckshot sinkers had scarcely taken the worms bottomward before the big red-and-green bobber started for China. Jeremiah felt a surging rush of power. The line pulled taut and the pole was bent almost double. Hope and sharp fear caught at his throat as the line ripped through the water.

"Hold him, Jerry!" Tildy shouted.

"Keep a tight line, son," Hiram warned.

"It's the Big One," Jerry gasped. "You take him, Uncle Hiram."

"He's yours, Jerry."

"I'll lose him sure as shootin'. He's arunnin' for the snag."

"Gotta land your own fish in this world," Hiram said. "Stay with him, boy."

Upstream like a bullet, with the line fairly singing, then down, down in a long, clean dive for the sunken boulders and logs ten feet under the surface went the big silver catfish. "Dear God, don't let me lose him," Jerry prayed. "You know I've been adreaming about catching this whopper since 'way last spring. He's gettin' under the snag, God, and You've gotta help me ease him out."

Praying and almost weeping, Jeremiah fought the big fish until his arms ached. He was pulled knee-deep then almost hip-deep into the fast water while Tildy ran up and down the shore shouting madly.

"Stay with him, Jerry," Hiram said. "Stay with him, boy."

"I'm agonna land that cat iffen it takes me till

sunup," Jeremiah whispered. "And if God don't help me, I'll do it by my ownself."

Then suddenly, after a mighty surge, the line went slack, the pole snapped straight, and the great catfish was gone. The boy had prayed for his bull calf. He had prayed for help with this passionately longed-for catfish. It must be like Granny said, prayers for things of the flesh are never answered.

Fighting to keep back the tears, Jerry waded ashore.

"You got another hook, Uncle Hiram?"

"That's the spirit, son."

But Tildy was openly weeping as they dug for more worms. And even when Jeremiah had safely landed a two-pounder, they all felt a little sad. Jerry had hooked into the Big One. He had held his line tight and played the fish expertly. Maybe you couldn't expect to see Dan Patch and catch the biggest catfish in Blue Lick River all on the same day.

Granny was curiously gentle with Jeremiah when they drove into the yard at the cabin in Cat Hollow. She had finished Jeremiah's spading, a quiet way in which she sometimes rebuked him. But she had been thinking back to another April as she worked, and she had been more lonesome than angry when she found his well-worn copper-tipped shoes.

Uncle Hiram's cheerful voice singing:

> "Granny, Granny, where's your fryin' pan at?
> The bestest fish is silver cat.
> 'We'll have fish,' cried old Dan Tucker,
> 'Rolled in corn meal, fried in butter.'"

reminded Granny that she was aching for mortal companionship.

"Course you'll stay for supper."

"Promised Tildy's mother I'd get her home 'fore sundown."

"Thank you kindly just the same," Tildy said.

Uncle Hiram unloaded the cultivator. Jerry was sent to fill the woodbox while it was still light. Granny would

23

need hot water if the ewes should take it into their heads to have their lambs that night.

The jolt wagon disappeared into the blue haze of the April twilight with Uncle Hiram's voice coming faintly back:

> *"Plant your taters in the dark of the moon;*
> *Good-by, Granny, see you soon.*
> *Teched in the haid was old Dan Tucker,*
> *Passed up catfish for his supper."*

An evening star appeared above the horizon. The first whippoorwill began deep in the Tarleton woods. And so ended an April day in the year of Our Lord, nineteen hundred and three.

2 LAMBING TIME

The lambs did not come that night nor the next, although the udders of the ewes were swollen with milk and their flanks were concave with desire to bring forth their young. Granny Kincaid (who had been Samantha to her David) ached and fretted for them as though she herself were about to bear child. She knew without consulting her calendar that the five months had neared their climax. The restless ewes stood glassy-eyed in their deep-strawed pens, complaining softly; nor would they touch their grain with more than tentative lips.

They were the daughters of daughters of daughters of the sheep David had raised with his own gnarled hands, and as such they went back through generations of begetting to the three beloved ewes dropped in the Cumberland far away and long ago (almost the sum total of the worldly wealth David had brought to his seventeen-year-old bride when the two were wed in Laurel Gap two years before the Civil War).

Jeremiah knew little of his Grandfather David, who had died in an April such as this three years before Jerry's unwanted birth. And Granny Kincaid, who had her own curious way of reciting history and framing

25

parables, was only now approaching the moment to enlighten her young charge. She had so interwoven her life with the loom (and the Bible) that all her most engrossing stories were first meticulously fashioned into covers, then supplemented by ballads of her own improvisation, sung to music which she herself composed upon the dulcimer.

> "David was Jesse's youngest son
> (The fiddlin', singin', zitherin' one);
> A shepherd lad who tended sheep
> (You gotter be brave with sheep to keep).

> "Faith, faith—
> You gotter have faith—
> The Good Book saith
> You gotter have faith."

Now with the April rain sweeping in torrents across the dark roof of the cabin and with Jeremiah safe abed in the loft, Granny sat at her loom weaving the story of the biblical David, who was also somehow Jerry's father's father—the David Kincaid whom Samantha had so boldly taken at candle-popping time in the blue dusk of a Cumberland April. And if Josiah Tarleton, who had also craved Samantha's hand, had somehow become the Goliath of the story, that too was understandable.

Among the people who read only one book it is not surprising that life sometimes parallels the Bible.

> "The stormy night was dark and cold,
> The big bears growled and the wolves were bold;
> All that he had was a little ol' sling
> But he potted them varmints on the wing.

> "Faith, faith—
> You gotter have faith—
> The Good Book saith
> You gotter have faith."

The closely threaded warp on the loom made a pattern of fine shadows, delicate and regular, upon the bare, white-scrubbed pine floor. The tracery trembled by coal-oil lamplight like a honeysuckle vine in an evening breeze. And through this vine the shuttle sped back and forth like a frightened hummingbird.

Yes, David had been young and shy, Josiah overweening and bold. But Samantha had not waited for one boy or the other to take her hand at the moment of troth when the light of the candle found the hidden pocket of gunpowder in the tallow. It was unseemly for the girl to do the choosing. But as the startling little explosion snuffed the candle and pairs of lovers plighted, Samantha had rushed to David's arms. And the gigantic Josiah (who could offer her frocks and lands and the old stone mill on Laurel Creek) had stormed out into the April evening.

Who was David Kincaid save the penniless shepherd boy who tended the Tarleton sheep? What had he in the world but the three ewes given him by Josiah's father in payment for his labor? Who had anointed this David's head with oil that he dared to plight his troth to Samantha? Would not the great young Tarleton, whose massive arms were like weaver's beams, crush this brash young shepherd?

> "Goliath had both heft and height,
> You never seed such a scary sight.
> Taped six cubits and a span—
> Ear-chewin', eye-gougin', real mean man.

> "Faith, faith—
> You gotter have faith—
> The Good Book saith
> You gotter have faith."

Josiah Tarleton waited for David in the dusk of Laurel Gap. And there they fought for hours until both were near death. Samantha and David were hurriedly wed—she remembering the words from Ruth, "For whither thou goest, I will go; and where thou lodgest, I will lodge; thy people shall be my people, and thy God my God." And they fled north into Indiana with their three ewes, little suspecting that Josiah Tarleton would follow.

Yes, thought Granny Kincaid, as she sat weaving by lamplight, awaiting the remote but direct offspring of those ewes, the time was approaching to tell Jeremiah the stormy story of his ancestry.

This being the third night since Granny first expected the lambs, her ears were attuned to some vibration almost above the human ear. It was scarcely possible that either she or Jeremiah could have heard the ewes bleating in such a storm. Yet now she raised her head to listen, and now his tousled head appeared at the loft hole, his eyes blinking in lamplight.

Jeremiah did not know what had awakened him. Certainly it was not the rush of rain and wind across the shingles above his four-poster in the loft—the wild lullaby which has soothed every loft child since the first cabin was built in the American wilderness. The feather bed of goose down atop the witch-hazel mattress had never felt softer, and the "Walls of Jericho" coverlet over him gave him the protection not only of its wool but also of the spirit of Joshua for whom the walls came tumbling down.

He lay wide-eyed in the darkness listening to the soothing rhythm of Granny's loom making him a story kiver of David and Goliath. And at last, when it seemed that sleep would never come, he went to the rectangle of lamplight in the floor and peered down the loft hole.

He heard Granny mutter to herself, "Tonight's the night. I kin feel it in my bones." It wasn't the first time in her sixty-one years that Samantha Kincaid had midwifed a lambing.

"The night for what?" Jeremiah asked sleepily, but deep in his marrow he already knew.

"Land of Goodness, child! You still awake?" She turned from her loom, her eyes sweeping the beamed and herb-draped ceiling of the great room, seeking the lamplit face of the awakened boy.

"Try countin' sheep, Jeremiah."

"I been acountin' sheep, Granny. New lambs mostly."

"Tonight's the night."

"For the lambs to come?"

28

"At the stroke of midnight," said Granny Kincaid. "It's most usually a mean, raw, blustery night like this." And just at that moment the old clock on the mantel began to strike the witchy hour of which she had spoken.

He was afraid she would not let him go with her through the rain to the pens where the ewes were quartered. And in truth she was wondering if the time had yet come to teach him the mysteries of birthing—the cruel secrets, wet with mortal gorm and agony, when the gentle mothers strained to bring new and innocent life into the world. Granny did not know that Jeremiah had already watched Blueberry bring forth the bull calf she had sent to slaughter—had helped the deep-voiced mother dry her bawling offspring. Jeremiah had only told his grandmother that he had found the calf in the far corner of the pasture—a small deception for which his conscience suffered. It was this secret and the aid he had given which had doubled his love for the brown-eyed bullock (now dead and lost to him forever). It was like every other pet he had ever had: there was no place for useless creatures on so poor a farm. He could see Granny lighting the lantern and warming the cotton flour pokes before the fire.

"Reckon the lambs are borned yet?"

"Cain't be no bornin' without a granny woman," chuckled the spry old lady.

"I could hold the lantern," Jeremiah said wistfully.

"Wal." Granny hesitated.

"I'm a big boy," Jerry said. "My innards ain't the least bit queasy."

"Wal," Granny said, "I reckon. But put on your boots and bundle up tight."

"Yes, ma'am," said Jeremiah, tearing down the ladder in flying nightshirt and leaping into his homespun jeans and shirt. "Hurry, Granny, they'll all be borned."

"In the Lord's good time," said Granny. "Now don't forget your jacket."

Head into the wind, they beat their way toward the barn, the lantern making a luminous room hollowed from the black infinity of wind and rain. Raindrops

29

hissed against the lantern, blurring and deflecting the yellow light. The wet elms soughed in the wind, tossing shadowy branches toward the unlit heavens—their voices mournful; the shadows of their boles lengthened gigantically across the rain-swept fields. Wet boulders huddled like drenched animals along the muddy lane. The golden mushroom of straw ballooned to unpredictable girth; and from its shelter lantern-dazzled sparrows tumbled blindly into the storm. The light quavered on the pools of rain water in the muddy ruts.

It took the strength of both the woman and the boy to open the barn door against the wind. Like the crack of a great whip the door slammed shut behind them. Suddenly they were safe in the warm stable smelling pleasantly of dusty hay, whitewash, drowsy animals, and acrid manure. Big Andrew Jackson, the mule, drowsed in his stall. Blueberry, forefeet neatly curled under, turned in sleepy surprise, chewing her cud thoughtfully. She mooed a gentle greeting.

And there beyond the cow were the four sheep-pens where the miracle had already occurred. The eyes of the ewes, no longer glazed with inward looking, shone green-gold in the lantern light. And there, in the straw beside each mother, was a newborn, wet, tightly curled lamb. The ewes spoke softly, and with small voices the lambs answered—a conversation unneedful of words but richly understood.

"Four new lambs," Jerry said.

"Mainly joyous and pert," said Granny.

Not one was stillborn. Not one was bewitched with the dreaded cowl of membrane over its head. Granny had reason to fear that this would be no ordinary crop of lambs, for ever since they had seen that wild, stray ram break through the tumble-down pasture fence in the autumn dusk of the previous November, Samantha had nursed an unreasoning fear. If that were the Tarleton ram, these lambs might be as full of devils as the swine of the Gadarenes pitching themselves down that steep place into the sea to perish as mentioned in the Gospels. No good thing could come from the Tarleton farm where the mistress of witch-

30

crafts had once lived and where a poplar tree now grew from her corpse in the neglected family plot.

No lamb bewitched or ill-formed. It was indeed a miracle. The Lord had rewarded Granny for dipping and drenching and feeding and protecting her flock. Lilith Tarleton from her grave had not prevailed. Samantha's lips caressed the admonition in Deuteronomy which once again had protected her household—the words chastising any mortal "that maketh his son or his daughter to pass through the fire, or that useth devination." Had not Lilith been "an observer of times, or an enchanter, or a witch, or a charmer, or a consulter with familiar spirits, or a wizard, or a necromancer?"

All these were still an abomination unto the Lord. And did it not say in Exodus, "Thou shalt not suffer a witch to live"?

Granny was called from her dark thoughts by the voice of Jeremiah shouting happily: "Aw, Granny, look! Jezebel's got twins."

"Black as Satan and as ugly," Granny said, the fear returning in full measure.

"I think he's purty," Jerry said, drying the lamb gently with a clean flour sack. "Look, Granny. He ain't a bit afeared."

But Samantha was not surprised to discover that the lamb was already an outcast. Huddled in a far corner of the second pen, shivering and alone, this small pariah had already found the world surprisingly cold and unfriendly. Unlike his twin sister, he was jet black with cinnamon leggings and a wicked and wonderful little face. Jeremiah thought that never in his life had he seen anything so beautiful as that little black buck lamb.

"She won't have him," said Granny, wise in the ways of sheep. "Even Jezebel won't suckle him."

"Maybe she'll have him," Jerry said. "I'm agonna try."

He lifted the lamb in his arms and crossed to the ewe who lowered her head menacingly and hooked at the boy sharply with her small horns. Her eyes glowed fiercely in the lantern light.

31

"Like mother like son," said Granny. "Bad blood on both sides."

Jerry remembered with a tingle of fear along his spine that Granny thought Jezebel was bewitched (ill-tempered and wayward, often breaking through fences and wandering Lord knew where—bleating in the night like a thing possessed). In the Bible it said that dogs would eat the flesh of the witch, Jezebel. And it was a wonder this ewe had so long evaded her fate. Granny had said last autumn, when the strange ram came courting, that Jezebel must have lured and enchanted him into the pasture.

Lilith Tarleton must be laughing out there in the wind and the rain to see Jeremiah already in love with this little devil lamb.

"Help me hold her, Granny."

"Hold still, you torn-down scoundrel," Granny cried, struggling to quiet the ewe while Jerry put the eager mouth of the black lamb to the dripping teat.

"Hold her, Granny."

"Hold still, you consort of Satan," Granny whispered, "you gimlet-eyed, onnatural beast."

But the ewe would make no compromise with her second child. Breaking away from Granny, she turned and bunted the lamb halfway across the pen. He folded up like an accordion in the straw, but he did not bleat pitifully as another lamb might have done. Already a spark of independence and pride was stirring in his blunt-nosed fleecy head.

"It's no use, son," Granny said.

"But he'll die."

"Good riddance," Granny said with surprising bitterness.

"Iffen we put a little ewe's milk on his head . . ." Jerry began.

"Won't make a particle of difference," Granny said. "She's bound and determined."

"He's shakin' and shiverin'," Jerry pleaded. "He's scairt and he's hongry. We ain't agonna just let him die, are we?"

"Old black buck lamb."

"He cain't help it iffen he's black."

"Cain't help it don't mend it."

"Nothin' to eat, nowhere to go, nobody to love him, he'll die, Granny."

" 'The Lord giveth and the Lord taketh away,' " Granny said. " 'Blessed is the name of the Lord.' "

Jeremiah knew that Granny could be hard as flint when she had a mind to say "No." She always had the Lord God Almighty on her side either way she argued. Sometimes, as now, Jeremiah felt like striking out against them both.

"The Lord don't care," Jeremiah said. "He ain't even looking."

"Jeremiah," Granny said, "you're blasphemin' again. He even heedeth the sparrow's fall. He is your shepherd and mine. That lamb is nestled in the palm of His hand." Then she added more gently, "Memorize the Twenty-third Psalm?"

"Yes, ma'am, I memorize," Jerry said, biting his lip to keep back the tears. And while Granny was putting more straw in the other pens he began saying softly to himself, " 'The Lord is my shepherd, I shall not want' . . . yer a mighty fine leedle black buck lamb . . . 'He maketh me to lie down in green pastures, He leadeth me beside the still waters' . . . and I've got a name all picked out for you: Danny; you like that name, little feller? It's after Dan Patch, a pacer that can skitter around the mile in less than two minutes. There, yer gettin' warmer, ain't you?"

Granny didn't see him tiptoeing out of the pen and toward the door.

"Jeremiah."

No answer.

"Jeremiah, bring the lantern."

No answer.

"You heered me. . ."

But the boy and the lamb had slipped out into the night.

Did it not say in Proverbs: "He that spareth his rod hateth his son? But he that loveth him chasteneth him

33

betimes"? And had not Jeremiah disobeyed her twice within the week, first running off to Fulton Corners to feast his eyes on that sinfully beautiful race horse, and now stealing away with the forbidden lamb? Because she loved him, she must chastise him. She took the lantern from the oaken peg where Jeremiah had hung it and went out into the night in search of a willow switch.

A great rift had been torn in the clouds and the storm was over. The heavens indeed proclaimed the glory of God, showing His handiwork. It flashed across Granny's mind that "Lo, the winter is past, the rain is over and gone." But the mood did not last. It was because she had spared the rod on her own Seth, son of David and father of Jeremiah, that he had lived to shame her; for as it said in the Scriptures: "The rod and reproof give wisdom; but a child left to himself bringeth his mother to shame."

At the corner of the springhouse she tore a stout switch from the willow tree, and, pulling it through her work-calloused hand, stripped the tender new leaves and catkins from its supple green length. "Correct thy son and he shall give thee rest; yea, he shall give delight unto thy soul."

But as she stepped into the big room of the cabin where she had been both mother and father to Jeremiah since cradle-rocking days; where she had taught him his first word and knitted his first garment, her heart almost misgave her. There in the pool of lamplight on the wide hearth Jeremiah had made a bed for his lamb in the hickory-splint kindling basket, lining it as best he could with warm flour pokes and dishcloths.

Steeling herself for the thrashing, she said, "Jeremiah, it's my bounden duty to chastise you. Take down your pants."

Jerry drew the lamb closer and looked up with pleading eyes as Granny put the lantern on the warming oven.

"You heered me, Jeremiah." She tapped the whip menacingly on the palm of her left hand.

"I'm ready for my lickin', Granny," the boy said,

"but please kin I warm and feed this little feller first?"

"Tryin' to git around me, ain't you?"

"Ain't never run away from a switchin' yet," the boy said with quiet pride.

"That's the Gospel truth," Granny admitted.

"Honest, Granny, you kin whop the livin' daylights out of me. But please—he's hongry and cold. You gotta help me."

"Wal," Granny said, hanging her shawl on its hook, "you got it comin' and yer agoin' to get it 'fore you go back to bed. Furthermore, I'm aputtin' my foot down and you ain't agoin' to keep that lamb."

"But first, Granny . . ."

"Oh, all right. Suppose I'll have to lend a hand." She placed the switch within easy reach on the table.

From the battered copper teakettle singing on the range she poured a dishpan of hot water, cooled it from the water pail, and tested it with her bared elbow.

"Won't have the little devil on the place. Eatin' his haid off. Bustin' through fences."

"Look, Granny, he's real gentle. See, he's suckin' my finger."

"Ornery old black ram."

"Black sheep give the most wool, Granny."

"Fiddlesticks," said the old lady, rummaging in the cupboard for funnel, bottle, and one of Jeremiah's baby nipples. "Stuff and nonsense."

"Says so in a pome they learned me at school:

> " 'Black sheep, black sheep,
> Have you any wool?
> Yes, sir! Yes, sir!
> Three bags full.' "

"That's a right smart passel o' wool," Granny scoffed. "Don't rightly recollect three bags full offen any sheep I ever seed sheared."

"It stood in a book. That's what the pome said."

"It don't stand in the Good Book," Granny said, pouring milk into a saucepan on the range. "Pomes is mostly purty words."

"Aw, Granny. You kin make me a black homespun shirt."

"Never keered for old black wool offen an old black buck sheep."

"Look, Granny, he's feelin' real pert! He's gonna be the biggest ram in Fulton Township."

"Looks real puny and ailin' to me. Here, dip him in this warm water."

"Oh, thank you kindly, Granny. . . . Look, he likes it. . . . I'll feed him clover. He'll get so big and fat and strong."

"And mean and ornery," Granny added, "full of vinegar and pizen. Dry him with this flour poke, Jerry. His bottle's ready."

She tried the milk for temperature again, sprinkling a few drops expertly on the back of her hand. Jerry saw with his own unbelieving eyes that Granny herself offered the eager lamb the nipple. The small, clean, cloven-hoofed baby pulled with joy upon the rubber teat, his tail whirling like a windmill.

"Where would you be keepin' him?"

"Here in the kitchen."

"How you gonna feed him?"

"Bottle-feed him on this here bottle."

"Whatcha goin' to name him?"

"Danny."

"Funny name fer a lamb."

"It's a wonderful secret name. Oh, Granny, please?"

"I reckon."

"You reckon you will?"

"I don't reckon I won't," said Granny; "leastways till he's big enough to roast."

"Oh, Granny. Yer the best granny," Jerry said, kissing the wrinkled cheek which just now had a salty tear upon it. "Give me my lickin' now, 'cause I won't hardly feel it I'm so happy."

"Bother," said Granny, breaking the willow switch and throwing it into the fireplace. "I'm gettin' softer'n beeswax." She wiped her eyes on a corner of her gingham apron.

36

3 THE SHEARING OF THE SHEEP

It seemed to Samantha that since the creation of the world there had been sheep to shear in the month of roses and blue spiderwort. Summer had followed spring up the river valleys, turkey-tailing out into every run and fork. The hedgerows ran amuck with bloom, and quail called their cheerful "Bob White" from snake fences so gray and venerable that Lincoln might have split their rails. Pastures were suddenly washed with the white-and-yellow foam of oxeye daisies blooming in countless millions. Wild strawberries were ripe. For the sixty-first time in her life the earth had encircled the sun, and the season for the shearing of the sheep had come again.

Samantha's years lay all in one vessel, like the rose petals she put down with layers of spices and herbs. Not all had moldered into an aroma to pleasure the nostrils. Some were as bitter as aloes. It was at sheep-shearing time that Josiah Tarleton had arrived from Kentucky to start building his new stone mill on the adjoining land up Bean Blossom Creek. David, whose back had been permanently twisted in his fight with Josiah, felt the dark menace washing down the valley like an icy wind (although the month was warm). Not only had Samantha's other swain followed the crippled young shepherd northward, but he had found it in his heart to flaunt his wealth almost within sight of their cabin by damming the creek and building his substantial mill and house of stone. Flashing by in his smart rig behind his team of prancing black horses, he was a living reminder of their poverty (and what Samantha might have had in worldly goods had she married David's mortal enemy).

And when, in the passage of time, the huge, dark-browed Tarleton had married Lilith, matters became worse rather than better for the Kincaids. David had quietly scoffed at Samantha's theory that the lung worms and stomach worms and inexplicable hemorrhages which killed their sheep were caused by a spell cast by that witch and enchantress, Lilith. But another dark occurrence at sheepshearing time had shaken even David from his logical moorings.

Samantha would remember till the day they lowered her into her bury hole how she had seen from the cabin the wall of water rushing down Bean Blossom Creek to the summer-shallow pool where David was washing his sheep for the shearing. Who but Lilith could have opened the great floodgates in the milldam in an attempt to murder both the shepherd and his sheep? Three ewes were drowned in that flood. David himself had barely managed to swim to safety. Even now, when Lilith lay entwined with poplar roots in her curious coffin, Samantha hated and feared her as she hated and feared Lilith's daughter Arabella (also in her grave), and Arabella's brother, the gaunt and voiceless Lafe. While Lafe still lived, Samantha would do her utmost to keep Jeremiah from trespassing upon Tarleton land.

She had tried to tell all these early phases of the ancient feud to Jeremiah in a sort of parable before he himself went into the sheepshearing pool this June. She had completed her story kiver and her ballad in

38

an attempt to teach him reverence for his grandfather and for the biblical David—a sermon concerning the need for courage when small men must stand against the great. But Jeremiah's less tortuous mind, wrestling with Granny's hints and parables, was still somewhat confused. Often in his dreams he mistook his grandfather for the David in the Bible. Cat Hollow was somehow the Holy Land. And Blue Lick River, the Jordan. Granny herself had intertwined the two.

Sheepshearing time again. And Jeremiah had at least been warned that should a wall of water come down the creek while he and Uncle Hiram were in the pool he must swim for his life.

Yes, June was upon them with its warm rush of full leaf and blossom. And Jeremiah, only lightly touched by Granny's memories and ballads, was drunk with the juice of living. Often he tried for the Big One with his Calcutta pole; returning invariably with smaller but still-welcome fish. School could not keep in such a season. Slates and *McGuffey's Readers* were put away until October. After the chores were done and the hoeing finished in the garden Jeremiah had hours to play with his black lamb.

From the first, Granny had been right in her prediction. It was less than a week before the lamb had learned to tip over his hickory-splint basket—to race around the cabin, leaving a shambles behind him. He nibbled and trampled and begged for his bottle. Soon he was following Jeremiah everywhere like a small, mischievous dog. The two had a game they played. Jerry would get down on his knees and they would butt their heads together like young twin billy goats.

"Feisty and fractious," Granny complained; "wild and wicked as newborn foals."

If you happened upon Danny sleeping in the fore-yard, angelic as Lucifer before the fall, you would never suspect that the little black angel could become a little black devil quicker than you could say, "Get thee behind me, Satan"—tipping over milk pails, running riot through the flowers.

Granny was doing her washing while they awaited

Uncle Hiram on this bright Monday morning; and Danny had just tipped over the clothesbasket, spilling all the newly washed clothes.

"Git out of my wash, you hellion," Granny cried, running to the rescue.

The lamb, turning quickly to avoid her upraised stick, quite by accident knocked Granny's knees from under her. Jeremiah knew it isn't polite to giggle when folks are in trouble, but he was fairly bursting with laughter to see Granny lick-splitting after the lamb all through the rosemary, thyme, and tarragon of her yarb garden.

"Black rascal!" Granny shouted. But the lamb was not impressed. He was his own man, as independent as a hog on ice, and as full of fizz as applejack. He leaped high into the air with legs as taut as spring steel and went hot-footing up one row and down the other, with Granny, spry and angry, always at least three jumps behind.

"Black scalawag," Granny cried, giving up the chase, "I'll tan yore hide next chance I git."

"Aw, Granny, he's just a poor brute-beast," Jerry pleaded. "He don't know he's wicked."

"Run fetch mint from the springhouse, Jerry."

"Whatcha want mint for, Granny?"

"Mint sauce, that's what for."

"Whatcha fixin' to roast, Granny?"

"Spring lamb, that's what I'm fixin' to roast."

"No," Jerry said fiercely. "You ain't ever agoin' to lay a hand on Danny."

"Happen he dumps my Monday wash again, I'll roast him," Granny promised. "I'm jist about mad enough to eat that critter raw."

"Think she meant it?" Jeremiah asked Uncle Hiram when he arrived later that day to shear the sheep. They were walking down the lane to the pasture with Danny frisking in circles as they strode along.

"Cain't tell about your granny," Uncle Hiram said, pulling thoughtfully on his corncob pipe. "Sometimes she barks big and bites little, and then again she's a ring-tailed roarer. I remember one time . . ."

And Hiram was off on the story of how Granny lay in wait for Lilith Tarleton soon after the cascade of water had been sent down on David and his sheep. Lilith, it seemed, had been light-footed and fancy-free, always roaming the woods and fields in fine or stormy weather, day or night, moonlight or starlight, as airy as a specter hound and in Samantha's mind as dangerous. Granny had been bound and determined that Lilith would never again put a spell on the Kincaid sheep. So she lay in wait behind a clump of hazel bushes in the pasture and when Lilith came singing down Bean Blossom Creek, fairly floating over the rail fence, David's wife had stoned her out of the pasture, calling upon Jehovah to be her witness that here was a witch and an enchantress.

"Your granny's got it all figured out," Uncle Hiram said, "that since the days of Cain and Abel the Lord's been on the side of the shepherds."

"I know," Jerry said, " 'cause Abel was a keeper of sheep and his wicked brother Cain was just a tiller of the soil."

"You might use that agin Granny next time she wants you to hoe in the garden." Uncle Hiram chuckled. Not that either of them imagined they could outquote Granny in a knock-down, drag-out, no-holds-barred, Scripture-quoting contest.

"On the side of the shepherds," Uncle Hiram said, lighting his pipe again. " 'Specially on the side of the shepherd David." And he began singing the opening verses of Granny's "David and Goliath" ballad.

"I disremember," Jeremiah said, "what happens after Samuel comes and anoints David's haid with oil."

"Wal," Hiram said, "I disremember that verse too. But it might go something like this:

" 'Off to court went curly head
        A-ridin' on a burro with a loaf of bread;*

41

> *Met some robbers on the King's Highway*
> *'Zing' went the sling ('cause crime don't pay).*

> " *'Faith, faith—*
> *You gotter have faith—*
> *The Good Book saith*
> *You gotter have faith.' "*

Jerry started laughing so hard he had to double up on the grass. It wasn't that way in the Bible, but Uncle Hiram's new version was much funnier, so he begged for more verses. Hiram sat down on a stump and gave rein to his fancy, while Danny cavorted through the clover:

> *"Come to the Jordan, broad and deep,*
> *Too big a crick fer a feller to leap,*
> *Feet was afreezin' and his laigs was numb;*
> *But he had to swim it, so he swum."*

"Jist like that time my grandsir almost got drownded by Lilith Tarleton," Jerry said. "He had to have faith when that wall of water came roarin' down Bean Blossom."

"Positively," Uncle Hiram said; "faith and good works."

"Reckon the Jordan was as big as Blue Lick River?" Jerry asked. "I'd be afeared to swim it; I don't confidence them deep holes below the riffles. Maybe iffen I had more faith . . ."

"You gotter have faith," Uncle Hiram said, "but *also* you gotter know how to swim. Now your grandpap could do most everything young David in the Bible did—his back were a mite twisted but he were as brave as a lion.

> " *'David he were a feisty youth,*
> *A fightin' feller, and that's the truth;*
> *Philistines or Moabites,*
> *When it come to fightin', he liked fights!' "*

"Faith, faith," sang Jerry, "keep agoin', Uncle Hiram. Look, even Danny is alistenin'."

42

And so, remembering some of Granny's verses and making up others of his own, the big man sat in the cool shade smoking his pipe and singing to the boy and his lamb, having no particular desire to begin the hard job of washing and shearing the sheep. They might have been sitting pleasuring themselves under a fig tree in the days of David. The flock grazing just beyond them was like every such flock since the beginning of the world. These might have been Abraham's sheep or David's, returning to the fold at night, called forth in the morning, each by name, to pasture in the wilderness, coming at midday to a stream of living water to drink. It was in such a cup in the hills, perhaps, that David had learned to stand alone against great odds.

> *"Goliath had both heft and height,*
> *You never seed such a scary sight.*
> *Taped six cubits and a span—*
> *Ear-chewin', eye-gougin', real mean man."*

Now Jerry was fairly shouting the chorus, as much to keep up his own courage as to encourage little David; as much to protect his grandfather fighting for Granny's hand back there in Laurel Gap as to help with the downfall of wicked old Josiah Tarleton:

> *"Faith, faith—*
> *You gotter have faith—*
> *The Good Book saith*
> *You gotter have faith."*

"Wal," said Uncle Hiram, "it was quite a fracas. I mighta been afeared of Goliath my ownself—monstrous big feller all duded up in a bright red coat of mail; voice like thunder; made the earth shake like crab-apple jelly when he stomped his foot."

"I could lick Fud Grundy," Jerry said. "I got faith."

"Course you could lick Fud Grundy," Uncle Hiram agreed. "And you *gotter* have faith, but *also* you gotter beat the other feller to the punch."

"Go on, Uncle Hiram, sing about Goliath. I ain't afeared."

> *"Big brass helmet on his head,*
>   *Coat of mail that was red as red.*
>   *Greaves of brass on both his legs,*
>   *Big around as sorghum kegs.*

> *"Had a spear like a weaver's beam;*
>   *Shield so big it'd dam a stream;*
>   *He hollered 'n' bellered with all his might,*
>   *'Send some feller out to fight.' "*

The scene was suddenly so painfully real to Jeremiah that he could actually make out the form of Goliath there in the great willow tree across Bean Blossom Creek; the clouds beyond were the host of the enemy. Jerry himself was David taking the mortally dangerous path down to the creek to find the five stones for the sling.

"I ain't afeared this time," Jerry said. "Faith, faith, you gotter have faith . . ."

"Be sure you got your sling all set and ready," Uncle Hiram cautioned, relighting his pipe. "Goliath looks kinda big today; he's still ashoutin' fer a match—mighty sure of himself, seems like."

"Go on, Uncle Hiram. I'm ready."

> *"Israel's army heered them words*
>   *Skeered as a flock of leetle birds.*
>   *Up spoke shepherd David then,*
>   *'You fellers think yer fightin' men?'*

> *"Armed with sling and shepherd's crook,*
>   *Fotched five pebbles from the brook,*
>   *Knees was aknockin' and his jaw ajar;*
>   *Thar stood Goliath as big as a b'ar."*

The moment had come. Tense with excitement, Jerry joined in the chorus:

> *"Faith, faith—*
>   *You gotter have faith—*
>   *The Good Book saith*
>   *You gotter have faith."*

"He's amovin' around tryin' to get a better position," Jerry said, as the breeze swayed the big willow tree. "I don't confidence the way he's actin'. What's that he's hollerin', Uncle Hiram?"

"Cain't quite make it out," Hiram said, cupping his ear. "Seems like:

> " 'Skitter home, young'un, and mind yore sheep;
> Me, I'm takin' a snooze of sleep.' "

"He doesn't know pride goeth before destruction," Jerry said.

"Just a big dumb bully like Fud Grundy," Uncle Hiram admitted. "You kin lick him, son."

"What's he up to now, Uncle Hiram? Seems like he's laughin' real scornful-like."

> "Goliath laughed till he purty near died,
> 'You couldn't hit me iffen you tried.'
> David slung his leedle round stone
> Betwixt his eyes, right to the bone."

"Faith, faith——" shouted Jerry, leaping to his feet and doing a victory dance around Hiram followed by the dancing lamb.

> "You gotter have faith—
> The Good Book saith
> You gotter have faith."

"Dead as a doornail," Uncle Hiram said.

"Betwixt the eyes right to the bone," Jerry cried, gloating pridefully. Then he added with gentle sorrow, "I wouldn't want to kill anybody, would you, Uncle Hiram? I'd mourn it all the days of my life."

"I reckon that's Gospel truth," Uncle Hiram said. He began to sing the last verse softly and wistfully:

> "King David sat on a pure gold chair
> With a pure gold comb to comb his hair,
> Diamond banjer on his knee—
> Purtiest sight you ever did see."

45

Jerry always thought that the last verse really meant that his grandpap in heaven was sitting on a pure gold chair playing the diamond banjer. And it made him sad to think he had never seen the old man.

"Was Grandpap David like a king, Uncle Hiram?"

"Son," said Uncle Hiram, "your grandpap was poor and crippled; but he was truthful and unafeared. Yes, I reckon he was a king right to the marrow of his bones."

And now that the story was told Jeremiah and Hiram and Danny went down among the hills that might have been in the Holy Land to a stream of clear water, there to begin the shearing. And so a ceremony as old as mankind took place. Never before had the boy been trusted with the difficult job of helping to wash the sheep. It took strength and courage to hold them in the waist-deep pool while Hiram scrubbed them clean with a stiff brush. They bleated and struggled as though Jeremiah were trying to drown them.

"Giddy as geese," Uncle Hiram shouted above the splashing; "addlepated and twitterwitted."

"Whoosh!" cried Jerry. "Got a nose full that time."

"Stay with her, son."

"I'm astayin', Uncle Hiram."

One after another, in the ancient way since the beginning of time, the bleating and rebellious animals were pulled into the stream. Minnows nosed up the current, flashing in the sun, nibbling at Jeremiah's bare toes. And on the shore, dashing through fragrant sweet clover and Queen Anne's lace, Danny celebrated the shearing with wild exuberance—his young body full of sunshine and curiosity.

"Your turn next year," Jerry shouted at him.

The lamb answered him with a derisive "Baa"; he had not yet learned to be afraid of anything or anybody.

At last all four of the old ewes were shivering on the bank. Soon the warm Indiana sun was allaying their chill, and in less than two hours they were dry and beautiful. Hiram and Jerry, resting in the shade, talked of everything in the universe—of birds and woodchucks

46

and dulcimers and catfish. At last the shearing could begin.

Hiram was deft and gentle with the shears. He held each ewe firmly between his knees, removing the thick fleece in one unbroken blanket.

"See, Jerry? You gotta clip close, but you darsen't draw blood."

"You're the best sheepshearer in the world, I'll bet."

"World's a lot of territory."

"Wal, in Indiana then."

"Indiana's a purty big state."

"Wal, in Pike County, I'll bet."

"Pike's a right smart county."

"Wal," Jerry said, "anyhow in Fulton Township."

"Now yer talkin' plain common sense," said Uncle Hiram. "Course I'm the best sheepshearer in Fulton Township, 'cause I'm the only sheepshearer in Fulton Township. Help me with this fleece, Jerry. First you spread it out, skin-side down. Then you turn the sides in toward the center and start rolling from the breech end. There's a lot you gotta learn about this business if you want to be a shepherd like King David."

4 THE WARP AND THE WOOF

"I'm ararin' to make me a new counterpane," said Samantha Kincaid when they brought in the new fleeces. "Run, Jeremiah, and fetch me the cards."

Jerry knew that the "cards" were not the wicked squares of pasteboard with hearts and diamonds and clubs and spades upon them, rather a pair of big wooden-backed combs set with steel wire used by his grandmother to comb out the new wool into soft rolls of clean, straight fibers.

"Kin I card, Granny?"

"If you've a mind to," Granny said, smiling at the boy's clumsy efforts. "My land, a regular mare's nest. Jerry, you're all thumbs. Better help Hiram trim out the burs and tags; this here's woman's work."

A gentle madness seemed to seize her as she carded the wool; and a faint glow came into her weathered cheeks as she piled the loose rolls near her spinning wheel. There were weeks of work ahead spinning this wool into hard-twisted yarn, dyeing it in her dye pots, warping up the loom for her new counterpane, throw-

48

ing the fly shuttle countless thousands of times through the shed of the warp, and "inlaying," by finger-weaving, the imaginative figures of her improvised design.

"I've made me a 'Walls of Jericho' and a 'Young Man's Fancy,'" Granny said, more to herself than to Hiram and Jerry. "I've wove me a 'Tennessee Lace,' a 'Trailin' Vine,' and 'St. Ann's Robe'—I'm real tired of all them patterns."

"Do a story kiver, Granny."

"Jest what I was figurin' on doin'. Gonna preach me a sermon agin traipsin' women."

Uncle Hiram looked up quickly from the fleece he had laid out on the hearth.

"You ain't agoin' to do no sech thing, Granny; that ain't the way to tell the boy about his mam."

"Was my mam a traipsin' woman?" Jerry asked. "Tell me about her, Granny."

"Hush now," Granny said sharply. "And you mind your own business, Hiram Douglas. As I was sayin', I'll do me a story kiver that's a regular hell's-fire and brimstone sermon agin' traipsin' women."

"Now, Granny," Hiram pleaded, "let bygones be bygones."

"Never could abide traipsin' folk," Granny said bitterly. "You memorize in the book of Job, chapter one, verse seven, where the Lord said unto Satan, 'Whence comest thou?' and Satan sasses him right back and says, 'From going to and fro in the earth, and from walking up and down in it.'"

"Satan ain't the only traipsin' feller in the Bible," Hiram said (standing right up to the determined woman).

"That's plain Gospel," Granny agreed, "and every last one of 'em got into a peck of trouble. Israelites atraipsin' here and traipsin' there; forty years of traipsin' in the wilderness and what did it get 'em?"

"It got 'em the promised land," Jerry said.

"From the mouths of babes," said Uncle Hiram, laughing so hard the tears came into his eyes.

"Shucks and fiddlesticks," said Granny. "Have it your own way. But mind you, git all them burs out

49

of the wool. If there's anything I can't abide it's devil's
pitchforks in my yarn."

All that June day and the next Samantha Kincaid
carded wool as her own grandmother had carded it in
the Southern Highlands, and as her granny's granny
before her in the hills of Scotland. Far into the night
the spinning wheel turned. Late in the week she started
mixing colors in her dye pots, muttering to herself as
she stirred the brew. Samantha had no girl young'un
to teach the secrets of her art, so she commanded
Jeremiah to learn by rote every recipe stored in the
well-packed cupboard of her mind.

"Seems like this blue pot's been ayeastin' since allus-
ago," Granny said. "Bought my first indigo from a
peddler the year the Rebs fired on Fort Sumter; I remember it plain as yesterday. Your pap was asquawlin'
in his cradle; I gave him a sugar-tit the minute I
heered the peddler's bell. Now name it after me, Jeremiah: sour wheat-bran water, indigo, madder root, and
wood-ash lye. Keep your wits about you. What makes
the best blue?"

"Sour wheat-bran water," Jeremiah repeated duti-
fully, "indigo, madder root, and wood-ash lye."

"Peddler said Abe Lincoln'd never stand for seces-
sion—looked like war between the states. Peddler said
he didn't confidence our neighbor Tarleton. Turned out
he was right—regular copperhead, Josiah was—handsome devil but full of secesh. Now name me green
again, Jerry."

"Hickory bark and alum," Jeremiah recited. "Did
Grandpap go to the war, Granny?"

"He had a hurt back like I told you. Tried to enlist.
Hellbent to save the Union. But they wouldn't have
him."

"Did Josiah Tarleton go?"

"Paid a feller six hundred dollars to shoulder a gun
for him . . . now remember, walnut hulls for brown
. . . pokeweed and alum for crimson . . . sassyfras for
orange . . . touch-me-not for yellow."

"Yes, ma'am," Jerry said, "I memorize . . . Did
Morgan's Raiders ever git to Cat Hollow?"

50

"Come right up that there road; scariest sight you ever did see; ridin' the finest horses they could steal and kicking up a cloud of dust that purely ruined my Monday wash. Stopped overnight at Tarleton's. Your grandpap spied 'em out and purty near got caught. . . . Now when you get your blue pot boiling hard you dip a hank of yarn like this. . . ."

A narrow porch with a projecting shelter of roof ran the length of the Kincaid cabin. Protected from the rain but open to the summer air were the smooth oaken pegs driven into the walls of the house itself upon which Granny dried her newly dyed yarn. After dipping each hank into the boiling dye pots in the foreyard, she strung the yarn over the wide-spaced pegs, singing the ancient tragedy of Barbara Allen:

> "And out of his heart grew a red, red rose,
> And out of her heart a briar . . ."

Jeremiah could not understand the strange comfort old folks seemed to derive from the sorrowful story of the dead lovers. In his own heart it caused a wistful unrest somehow connected with the secret of his father and mother which Granny had so far been unwilling to reveal. But he loved to hear her fiddle-clear voice keeping time to her steps as she paced back and forth between the pegs:

> "They climbed to the top of the old church wall
> Till they couldn't climb no higher."

Munching Scripture cake (made with sweets all mentioned in the Bible), apleasuring himself with Danny beneath the trumpet vine, and listening to Granny sing while she spidered her bright web, Jeremiah was sad-happy as a mourning dove.

> "And tied themselves in a true lover's knot,
> The red rose and the briar . . ."

51

Meanwhile Granny Kincaid was thinking to herself that maybe she'd call her traipsin' woman kiver "Cat Hollow Wedding." She'd show the courtship, the infare, the wedding itself—and all the heartbreak that followed. She wondered if it would help her get shed of her hatred for Arabella Tarleton, or help to soften the loss of her only son, Seth, to weave it into a cover and put it all down in a ballad song. Of one thing she was certain—this was the right way to tell Jeremiah of his parentage. Tomorrow she would warp up the old walnut loom and begin her weaving.

5 STORE-BOUGHT TROUBLE

Jeremiah was deeply troubled as he and his lamb trudged down the road to Fulton Corners. Danny had been banished, first from the house and next from the foreyard (where he had managed to tip over a crimson dye pot). Granny Kincaid had hinted that the very next time the lamb gave trouble he would be sold to Mr. Turner.

Danny had proved that he could get through the tumble-down pasture fence as easily as a hot knife goes through butter. And Jerry could not bear to see his friend and playmate locked up in the barn. There seemed to be only one answer—a new, strong, woven-wire pen. Jeremiah had taken his small handful of pennies—all his worldly wealth—and was now headed for Pete Grundy's store.

"Gotta build you a fence horse-high, hog-tight, and bull-strong," Jeremiah told his lamb. "You're gettin' real mean and ornery, like Granny said."

Just then the lamb nuzzled softly at Jeremiah's pocket where he always carried a carrot or some other delicacy for his pet, so Jeremiah added, "You're wicked as sin, but I love you."

Jerry thought of all the peppermints and wintergreens and licorice whips and horehound drops he could buy with those pennies. But he put away the temptation. What he needed—what he absolutely must have—was at least ten yards of stout woven wire. Using a side of the barn for one side of such a pen and the thirty feet of wire for the other three sides, he would have an outdoor enclosure ten feet square—a prison, it was true, but a pleasant one for his pet.

"But suppose I don't have enough money," he mourned.

Danny seemed completely unconcerned. He was nipping red-clover blossoms and chewing them with delight.

"It ain't Christian to slaughter poor, dumb brute-beasts. They don't do nobody no harm. Oh, Danny, Danny," he said, "I hope I got enough cash money for the fence."

The bell tinkled when Jerry and the lamb walked into the general store.

"Get that critter out of here! This ain't no stock pavilion at the County Fair," the storekeeper shouted.

Grundy usually roared at children, so Jeremiah paid little attention. The checker players laughed lazily.

"Purty soon," Jerry said, "after I spend my money. He's a good lamb, Mr. Grundy; he won't cause no trouble."

"Wal, see that he don't," the proprietor grumbled, returning to his checker game while Jeremiah made a slow, delicious round of the store. There through the uneven greenish glass of the candy counter were all the mouth-watering peppermint sticks and mixed hard candies he must forego. No one had bought the four-bladed, stag-handled jackknife yet. And the sharp little hatchet with the red handle was still in its place. How could a man be mean who owned such a mountain of plunder?

Granny had told him never to touch things in the store, but he could see them and smell them: the fragrance of coffee beans, and pickled fish and cheese, and bacon. The eye-filling sight of bright steel saws,

54

smooth ax helves, and new pitchforks; the agonizing plenty of fishing tackle—hooks, sinkers, bright bobbers, new braided lines, and new poles.

Jeremiah was making his way slowly toward the corner where the fencing stood in tight rolls when he overheard one of the checker players say:

"Course that lamb's bewitched; Tarleton ram on one side, Kincaid ewe on the other——"

"Cat Hollow does funny things to folks and critters."

"Shhhh. The boy'll hear you. Probably don't know his granny on either side could make dogs have fits just by looking at 'em. Seen it many a time. . . ."

"Figger Granny Kincaid would cast a spell on her own black lamb?"

The men cackled with senile laughter, spitting tobacco juice into the box of sawdust. It took a Cat Hollow granny woman, they said, to make a dog foam at the mouth or bite the end off his own tail, make sheep go crazy in the dead of night, or a cow get the bloat. Like lamb, like boy—Kincaid blood on one side and Tarleton on the other. Rag, tag, and bobtail any way you figgered.

Jeremiah's heart was pounding so hard it seemed to echo in his ears. Momentarily the fencing was forgotten. He didn't see Fud Grundy hiding behind the flour barrel aiming his slingshot at Danny. Eyes cast down in shame, Jerry was listening, all unwilling and bewildered, to the talk of the old men.

"Come on, boy," said Pete Grundy, "make up your mind."

"Please, Mr. Grundy," Jeremiah began bravely.

"Please what? Speak up!"

"How much fence can you buy for thirteen cents? It's awful important . . ."

Jeremiah didn't get an answer. But he knew from the roar of laughter that he would never have enough money to buy the fence he needed; that Danny was doomed, and that the whole town was against him. Faith wasn't enough in this world, you *also* had to have cash money.

He was already wishing that he and Danny were

dead and buried side by side in the old graveyard when he heard the zing of Fud's slingshot. He saw his lamb leap in terror and start running wildly all over the store, tipping over racks of pans and skillets, bursting a bag of buckwheat flour (a white lamb, now), dashing madly into the back room and out again.

Pete Grundy picked up a broom. Panting and puffing, he gave angry chase.

"Go it, lamb, go it, Pete," shouted the delighted loafers around the cracker barrel.

"You're againin' on him, Grundy."

"Please," Jerry pleaded. "Don't hurt him."

"Sashay right and circle left," shouted one of the men, whipping out his harmonica to play a wild, shrill tune.

"Fud done it," Jerry shouted. "He shot him with his slingshot."

"You're a liar," Fud said.

"Take your partners, swing down the middle," called the wit at the cracker barrel.

"Head him off, somebody," Pete Grundy shouted. He swung his broom at the lamb, missed, and swept a whole row of cans off a shelf.

"Let me catch him," Jerry cried. "Please, Mr. Grundy."

The terrified lamb bolted straight for the screen door, tearing out a panel of rusted wire.

"Best dad-gummed circus since Bill Saunders' bull came to Methodist prayer meeting," said Grandpa Meeker, laughing so hard he nearly choked on his cut plug.

"And if you ever bring that black varmint into my store again," Pete Grundy shouted after Jeremiah, who had followed his lamb into the dusty street (startling the horses drowsing at the hitching rail and sending up a cloud of yellow butterflies from the mud puddle by the drinking trough), "I'll use a meat cleaver 'stead of a broom. Jest look at my screen door!"

"I'll get it fixed, Mr. Grundy," Jerry said. "But Fud done it. He shot my lamb with a slingshot."

56

"I'll take care of Fud," the storekeeper promised, returning grimly to assess the damage.

Uncle Hiram was a haven and a refuge in time of trouble. Working quietly among the shavings and sawdust of the big room adjoining the blacksmith shop, he seemed part of the sturdy materials from which he made wheels and looms and settin' chairs. But he was also akin to the dulcimers and fiddles hanging from the wall, the clean smell of pine and cedar, and the pattern of sunlight slanting through the dusty, many-paned windows. Hiram didn't turn from his bench as boy and lamb entered. He continued to fashion the new treadle for Granny Kincaid's loom.

"It weren't his fault," Jerry said. "Fud Grundy done it . . . And Granny ain't a witch, is she, Uncle Hiram? . . . And us Kincaids ain't rag, tag and bobtail . . . Oh, Uncle Hiram, I'm plumb miserable."

"Whoa there, young feller. Not so fast," said Hiram. "Now start clean back at the beginning and tell me all about it."

So Jerry told him what had happened at the store; what the men had said about his two grandmothers; and how Fud had shot the lamb with his slingshot, starting the whole shivaree. He poured his heart out on the subject of the threatened lamb, the need for a fence he could never buy, and the screen door he had promised to repair.

"Best way to mend things," said Uncle Hiram, "is a step at a time. I'll fix the screen door; and iffen you'll give me a few days' time I'll help you build a pen out of locust poles stout enough to hold an elephant."

"We got a whole bresh lot full of honey locusts," Jerry said.

"Next thing, I'll try to argue your granny out of sellin' the lamb to the butcher. 'Tain't goin' to be easy when she hears about the latest ruckus at the store."

"I'm that beholden," said Jeremiah, "it'd pleasure

57

me to work for you all the days of my life, free for nothin'."

"Shucks," said Uncle Hiram, "you ain't got no pap, and I ain't got no son . . . building a little old lamb pen's no trouble . . . only thing we got to worry about now is whether your two grannies are witches." He tousled Jerry's head with a big work-calloused hand.

Jeremiah's woebegone face had begun to show signs of an unmistakable grin; but a shadow of puzzlement still lingered. And Hiram decided it was high time to counter some of Granny Kincaid's tall stories, not to mention the mischief started by the loafers at the store.

"First thing," said Hiram, "there ain't no such thing as witches; there ain't no haunts or goblins or specter hounds neither. All a lot of poppycock. Furthermore, I knew your mother's mother, Lilith Tarleton. She weren't no more a witch than Granny Kincaid, who's purely on the side of the angels."

"Grandma Tarleton?" Jerry asked, trying it on his tongue. In all the times he had heard of the wicked Lilith he had never really thought of her as his grandmother.

"One of the finest women ever drew breath," said Uncle Hiram; "one of the purtiest too."

"I'd be much obliged," said Jeremiah, "to hear tell of Granny Tarleton."

So while the lamb basked in a pool of checkered sunlight on clean pine shavings, Jerry sat in a new hickory settin' chair listening to Hiram Douglas tell all he knew of Lilith Tarleton, born Lilith Henderson in Louisville, Kentucky, in the year of Our Lord, eighteen hundred and forty-seven.

"She loved birds and moths and flying creatures of all kinds," said Hiram; "sorta had wings herself, you might say . . ."

"But Granny Kincaid . . ."

"Sure, I know Granny Kincaid thinks . . . bound and determined Lilith was a witch while alive, and a haunt now she's dead; seen her diggin' plants in the woods that weren't dyes, yarbs or medicines—Samantha

58

Kincaid figgered they must be for witch's brew and potions; seen her running through the dusk with a long-handled net thing catching big moths—looked mighty peculiar to Samantha; heard her making bird-calls in the woods most any time of the day or night: hooting like an owl and calling like a whippoorwill . . ."

"What were she up to, Uncle Hiram?"

"Wal, son, some folks study books and some folks study God's green earth. Lilith's pap helped a feller named Audubon—right famous man, I reckon—helped him git all sorts of birds big and small so's this Audubon could paint pictures of 'em. Lilith's pap were just a stripling then, but he remembered what he learned, and he teached it to his daughter."

"It's a sin and a shame," said Jeremiah, "that Granny Kincaid ain't ever heered the truth about Granny Tarleton."

"I've been atryin' to tell her for nigh on thirty years," said Hiram. "She don't listen, or she don't understand, or she don't want to know—cain't quite figger it out."

But Hiram Douglas had his own theory about Samantha and Lilith, not one he could easily explain to Jeremiah. As he shaved neat curls of walnut from the treadle he was shaping, he thought back to the year he had worked at Tarleton's Mill on Bean Blossom Creek—admiring from afar Josiah Tarleton's bride. Josiah had never ceased to love Samantha Kincaid, and Samantha knew it, though she had put him forever out of her life. Lilith guessed the truth and turned to the woods and fields for her consolation. Hatred grew up between the women over the ever-more-surely owner of the mill. Young Hiram, just Lilith's age, mingled in none of their lives, save for his labor in the mill, yet he could not fail to sense the emotions running like heat lightning up and down the valley.

"In short," said Hiram, "you and your lamb come of real good stock on both sides of the fence. So hold up your head, young feller. Ain't nothing rag, tag, and bobtail 'bout either one of you."

"Thank you kindly," Jeremiah said; "and you figger

there ain't the slightest chance Granny Kincaid put a spell on my lamb?"

"Ain't no sech thing as a spell," Uncle Hiram said again, sandpapering the new treadle. "Just git them superstitious notions out of your head, Jerry. Don't make the least particle of difference if you plant 'taters in the dark of the moon or when it's big around as a green cheese. Iffen a cow won't let down her milk, there's some good reason for it. Iffen a dog or cat has fits, there's a reason for that too. I don't hold with potions, signs, or magic. A busted lookin' glass is just a busted lookin' glass. If a cock crows three times before dawn, it's on account of it wants to crow. Besides, it's only goats that has traffic with the devil, not black lambs."

"And Danny won't have fits and git puny and ailing?"

"He'll get big and strong and rambunctious."

"Oh, he's the best lamb," Jerry said, crossing to the shaving pile to throw his arm around his pet. "Folks just notice the bad things—nobody notices the good things he can do."

"For instance?"

"Wal, he can jump higher—and—and run faster than any lamb in Pike County. Iffen he was a horse, he'd be a world champion when he grows up."

"Now comin' up to the post," Uncle Hiram said in a loud voice, "Dan Patch and his namesake Dan Patch II . . .You wouldn't want him to beat old Dan Patch, would you?"

"How'd you know Danny's secret name? Even Granny don't know he's named for Dan Patch. She'd whop me, sure as shootin'."

"Wal, Jerry, there's a washin' machine in the dream book named for Dan Patch—does your wash in two minutes flat. There's a red-and-green sled named for that horse; and I jest figgered, seeing as how you're wearing that horseshoe-nail ring . . ."

"Uncle Hiram, horses win races and git to be champions. Then folks gotta admit they're wonderful. How

60

about things that don't race? How do they git to be champions?"

"What kind of things, for instance?"

"Well—like pigs and cows and roosters, for instance."

"Or maybe black lambs, for instance?"

"Uh huh," Jerry said, dropping his eyes and kicking shavings with a toe.

"Well, you take 'em to the County Fair, like that there ram of yours, and I'm the judge, for instance."

Uncle Hiram had finished the treadle and put it aside. He now assumed the pompous air of a livestock judge at the County Fair. Adjusting his imaginary glasses, he stroked his imaginary beard and said in a commanding voice:

"Over here, Mr. Kincaid—make him stand still while I look him over."

Jerry led the lamb a few feet and kneeled beside him with his arm around his woolly neck. Hiram shooed away two Plymouth Rock pullets that had wandered into the shop.

"Stand back, folks. Don't crowd now."

Hiram took an imaginary measuring tape from his overall pocket and circled the lamb with exaggerated caution.

"Keep a tight holt of that critter, Mr. Kincaid. Looks real ferocious."

"I got him, Jedge," Jerry said.

Hiram unwound the imaginary tape.

"Chest, six cubits and a span, just like Goliath."

"How much is six cubits and a span?"

"Wal, maybe ten or twelve feet," Uncle Hiram said. "Height to the shoulder, twenty-two feet four inches."

Jeremiah giggled.

"Open your mouth, you big brute-beast," Hiram said, "and don't chaw off my arm, neither. Hmmm, teeth like a buzz saw."

Hiram looked in the lamb's eyes.

"Mr. Kincaid, this here's quite an animal—quite an animal. Eyes like shooting stars. Fleece soft as goose down and thick as a mattress. Broad acrost the back as a lumber wagon. Kin probably outjump, outshoot, outrun, outfight, and outbrag any lamb in Pike County."

"No fooling, Uncle Hiram. What makes a lamb a champion?"

"Well, first, son, it's breedin'. You and I know Danny's daddy was probably a ripsnorter, and his maw, Jezebel, is a ring-tailed roarer, and he ain't a bad-lookin' critter himself. Course that don't give him a pedigree, as they call it. Folks'll just have to take his breedin' on faith."

"What else, Uncle Hiram?"

"Care and feedin'. Jest the right mixture of ground feed and lots of clover."

"But all the best clover is 'way down by the creek, and the pasture fence won't hold him."

"You'll just have to lead him on a rope, Jeremiah, into green pastures and beside the still waters till I can fix you a fence."

"Oh, I'll lead him into green pastures," Jerry promised. "Anything else I should give him?"

"Wal," Uncle Hiram said, "he needs a lot of love and affection. Can't hardly ever raise young champions without you love 'em."

He helped Jeremiah adjust a new length of rope with a knot that could not bind the lamb's neck, and started them off for their green pastures, amply rewarded by the look of happiness on the face of a boy who had so recently been miserable to the heart's core.

As Jerry went around a bend in the road near Tildy's house leading his lamb and whistling "Lord Randel," Fud Grundy and Archie McCoy stepped into his path. Fud had a green apple impaled on a stout willow withe, bent like a bow ready for action.

"Gimme your pennies," Fud said.

"Try and git 'em."

"Aw, we can git 'em," Archie said.

"Old blabber-mouth," Fud added.

"I ain't a blabber-mouth."

"You blabbed, and my paw whopped me."

62

"Had it coming and served you right."

"Come on, Archie, let's wreck his shanty."

"We're agoin' to knock your block off."

"I ain't afeared of you," Jerry said.

"He ain't afeared!" Fud groaned with simulated laughter.

"He's so afeared he's purty near wettin' his pants," Archie said.

"We're agoin' to cut your ears off and then we're agoin' to club your lamb."

"You leave my lamb alone."

"Your itsy-bitsy stinkin' old lamb," Fud said.

"Cat Hollow Kincaid," Archie said, circling to get Jeremiah's eyes into the sun; "clodhopper."

"Why don't your granny buy you store-bought britches?"

"It ain't none of your business what kind of britches I wear," Jeremiah said, tears of anger in his eyes. "I ain't a clodhopper. A Kincaid's good as a Grundy any day."

"Shinny on your tintype," Fud said; "go suck eggs, you egg-sucker." He pulled back his apple, ready to let it fly.

Granny had often told Jeremiah, " 'Tain't right to fight, but 'tain't brave to run." The Scripture said, "Do unto others as you would have them do unto you," and turn the other cheek, and a soft answer turneth away wrath. But it *also* said, "An eye for an eye and a tooth for a tooth." Granny finally decided you had to use plain common sense. Don't start a ruckus, but if the other feller starts one, whop the livin' daylights out of him. Young Grundy and Archie McCoy cheated at marbles. They took "pickings" and "cleanings" and "hunchings" when nobody gave them leave. They tied Jerry's clothes in knots down at the swimming hole in Blue Lick and shouted "chaw beef." Once they had held Jerry down and filled his mouth with mud. Three generations earlier their sort had gouged out eyes and chewed off ears all up and down the Ohio River Valley.

"Give it to him!" Archie shouted.

Fud sent the hard green apple whizzing through the air, clipping the lamb between the eyes. The small animal bleated, leaped against the rope, and struggled for freedom while Fud and Archie went into peals of laughter.

Jerry rushed at Fud, fighting with one hand while he held the rope with the other. Young Grundy backed away in surprise and pain as Jerry landed a stinging blow on his nose. But Archie jumped on Jerry's back, and soon the two bigger boys had him by the hair, pounding his face into the dust. They tried to get at the pennies in his pocket, and they tried to jerk the rope from his hands. But Jerry held on grimly, fighting them off as best he could, weeping silently.

Just at that moment Tildy rushed up, her cart banging along behind her.

"Bullies!" she shouted, "leave him alone! I'll hit you both with this stick!"

"You wouldn't dare," Archie said.

For answer Tildy started beating them with all her strength. The stick was large and stout and effective.

"Come on, Arch. We can't fight girls," Fud said, making a shamefaced retreat.

"Are you hurt bad?" Tildy asked Jeremiah.

"Aw, I'm all right," Jerry said, getting to his feet and starting off with the lamb.

"Wait, Jerry, I'm agoin' with you."

"Cain't wait. Got a job of work to do."

"What doin'?"

"Feedin' my lamb clover." He tried to wipe away the dirt and the angry tears that still were forming in his eyes.

"We'll get an extra cartful for Danny's breakfast."

"That's a plumb crazy idea."

"Please, Jerry."

So he let her come with him, following an old footpath which went by way of stiles and steppingstones cross-country toward Cat Hollow. And as they led the lamb and pulled the cart through meadows of clover, Jerry told her of his secret plan to take Danny to the County Fair. Even Granny couldn't have it in her

64

heart to slaughter a blue-ribbon, prize-winning ram; folks in Fulton Corners would never again call Danny Kincaid a rag, tag, and bobtail, good-for-nothing critter.

Tildy was big-eyed with wonder to hear Jeremiah talking of riding on the cars to a far city where the fair was held.

"Reckon Granny'll let you go?"

"Uncle Hiram can git around her."

"Your granny's awful stubborn sometimes."

"Uncle Hiram can wrap her around his finger like a white-oak splint."

"Let's play county fair," Tildy suggested. They had reached the place unbeknownst to anyone in the world except Jeremiah and Tildy. In the mouth of a wide, grassy ravine was a fairy mound, guarded by two ancient sycamores.

If you shut your eyes tight and counted to one hundred very slowly and then opened them just a crack you could see the little people and their little houses: granny women spinning and weaving on their tiny porches; jolt wagons no more than six inches long being pulled by gay little teams of horses perfect in every detail.

"Shut your eyes," Tildy said, "and I'll count: one, two, three, four . . ."

"Ain't ary a witch or specter hound or fairy in the whole world," Jeremiah said sadly, closing his eyes as he was bidden.

"Who said?" whispered Tildy fiercely; "ten, eleven, twelve, thirteen . . ."

"Uncle Hiram."

"Seventeen, eighteen, nineteen . . . Hush, they'll hear you."

"Will-o'-the-wisps ain't nothin' but fireflies."

"Little folks is different. I kin see 'em plain as plain . . . Twenty-one, twenty-two . . ."

"My grannies weren't never witches, and Lilith Tarleton ain't a haunt. And there ain't one little person on this here mound . . ."

"Hush, Jerry, hush. They're aputtin' up their tents and merry-go-rounds. They're acomin' with prize punkins and horses and black lambs . . . Thirty-one, thirty-two, thirty-three."

And sure enough, when they opened their eyes a crack there was the whole County Fair.

They could even hear the faint shouts of the little sideshow barkers and the whispered hoofbeats of the little race horses on the race track, while pennants as small as clover leaves fluttered on the breeze.

"I'm agoin' with you to that fair," Tildy said.

"I reckon, if you've a mind to."

It was the closest he could come to saying he was grateful for the brave way in which she had beaten Fud and Archie with her stick and conjured up this witchy world of little folk as real as any living thing that ever drew mortal breath.

Soon after Jeremiah had left the shop leading his lamb, Uncle Hiram had hitched his horse and jolt wagon and started for Cat Hollow. Delivery of the new treadle for Granny's loom was only an excuse; actually he had more important business on his mind. He thanked Samantha kindly for the Scripture cake and glass of milk she offered, but he would take no other pay for the treadle.

"Granny," he said, "you're too hard on Jeremiah."

"I reckon I can raise my own young'un as I see fit," said Granny sharply. She was working over a blending frame, using yarn from various-colored balls to make three strands into a single multicolored yarn.

"First place, he ain't your young'un," said Hiram, taking the bit in his teeth; "second place, he's a good boy who needs more love and less larrupin'."

"Ain't my young'un?" said Granny incredulously. "Like to know whose young'un he is if he ain't mine!"

"Seth's and Arabella's."

"Both amoldering in their graves," said Samantha. "God have mercy on their sinful souls. Next thing you'll be atellin' me, Seth wasn't my only son (lured to damnation by that traipsin' woman Arabella Tarleton)."

"Samantha," said Hiram wearily, "did you ever read

66

in the Bible where it says 'Blessed are the meek'? You ain't the only hard-workin', right-minded, God-fearin' woman on the face of the earth."

"I do my bounden duty accordin' to my lights," said Granny, starting a new blend. "I got calluses on my hands from workin' and calluses on my knees from prayin'. I've wore my old fingers to the bone araisin' that boy-child. Dragged him up from an orphan. And I ain't beholden to nobody for good advice."

"All Gospel truth, Samantha," Hiram conceded, "but you're holding the sins of the father and mother—always granting they *was* sins—against the innocent offspring."

"Spare the rod and spoil the child," Granny said. "I made my mistake in rearin' up a godless son; and I ain't aimin' to rear a godless grandson."

"I didn't say nothin'."

"Didn't say nothin' means you thunk plenty. You know as well as I do I gotter be hard as nails. I gotter be both mam and pap to that young'un. I gotter send him up the straight-and-narrer path to heaven, so's he won't go traipsin' down the wide primrose path to hell. And disobedience is one thing I won't tolerate."

"It ain't downright disobedience, Samantha."

"Like to know what you call it"—indicating with her head—"barn door's open, ain't it? Lamb's gone and so's the boy. That black scalawag leads him into temptation. It's rearin' up in the face of Providence to keep that critter around the place. Didn't see 'em down at the Corners, did you?"

"Yes," said Hiram with a sigh, "I did. And you might as well hear it from me. Lamb jest about wrecked Pete Grundy's store. But it weren't his fault. Fud Grundy popped him with a slingshot. . . ."

"Might of knowed," said Granny; "trouble, trouble, and more trouble. I gotter beat the Tarleton out of them two and preach the Kincaid into 'em. Pete sore?"

"Sore as a boiled owl." Hiram grinned.

"Served him right," said Granny. "Fud get a lickin'?"

"Pete tanned him proper."

"Wal," said Granny, "I'm glad that little black devil

got in one good lick afore I sent him to Mr. Turner."

"Samantha," said Hiram, "now I'm agoin' to talk cold turkey. You ain't agoin' to butcher that lamb. I fixed Pete's busted screen door. And 'fore the end of the week I'm afixin' a pen for Danny that'd hold the Saunders' bull. I never stood up to you yet for my ownself. You've said your say and had your way long as I've knowed you. But you ain't agoin' to break Jerry's heart and mine by murderin' that boy's lamb."

"Hiram," said Granny Kincaid, "I got my own cross to bear, and it ain't pleasurin' me none to send that lamb to the slaughter. Could I give you another piece of Scripture cake?"

"Thank you kindly just the same," said Hiram quietly. "Guess I'd better be gettin' along home. There ain't as much light as I thought out here in Cat Hollow."

6   A CAVE TO HIDE IN

That night after Jeremiah had gone to his bed in the loft, he lay listening to Granny talking to him from the room below. She had warped up her loom and had started her "Cat Hollow Wedding" cover, racking it with loud thumps to accentuate the points of her argument.

"Ain't one bit of use argufyin' with me, Jerry. I'm agoin' to sell that lamb to Mr. Turner in the mornin'. It's a pure mercy to the critter and a blessin' to Cat Hollow. You hear me, Jeremiah?"

No answer.

"Oh, you heered me, right enough. You jest won't give me the satisfaction. My patience is worn to a frazzle. I am like unto Job in the days of his affliction cryin' out upon the Lord. That no-good, torn-down scoundrel of a black buck lamb is the seven plagues of Egypt, and that's a fact. My mind's sot, and I don't want none of yore back talk."

No answer.

"Won't say 'Yes, ma'am,' won't say 'No, ma'am.' Sulky as a cornered varmint. Now you listen to me, Jeremiah Kincaid. It ain't just a question of that lamb askitterin' all over the place, bustin' and destroyin' things. It ain't what the lamb's adoin' to me or to Pete Grundy. It's what the lamb's adoin' to you. You hear me, boy?"

"Yes, ma'am."

"I been aspellin' out the Scriptures, seeking truth and guidance in the Good Book; and they did set up a golden calf and did fall down on their knees and worship it as an idol—and the Lord God turned his face *away* from them."

"Danny ain't a golden calf, Granny. He's a lamb."

"Lamb or calf, he's agettin' to be a heathen idol around here. And heathen idols must be cast down. You hear me, Jeremiah?"

"Yes, Granny."

"Wal, if the cat ain't got your tongue, why don't you say, 'Granny, yore plumb right; we gotter sell that no-good lamb'?" She racked her loom with violence, making the lamp chimney quiver and the shadows dance.

" 'Cause yo're quotin' the Good Book yore own way, same as always," came the small, determined voice from the loft. "It says in the Scripture, 'Follow the lamb whithersoever he goeth,' and that's what I aim to do."

"Quoting Scripture agin yore granny. Flyin' up in the face of yore elders and betters . . ."

"The Good Book's plumb full of shepherds watching their sheep in the fields by night," Jeremiah said, with quiet desperation, "and . . . and leading them into green pastures and beside the still waters, and ahuntin' for the lost one that is more precious than the ninety and nine. And it don't say one blessed thing about sacrificin' Danny."

"Don't say nothin' about givin' up a lamb? Why, boy, you're plain spittin' in the eye of Providence when you try to outquote yore granny who was suckled and teethed on the Holy Word. Why, the Good Book

70

is cram-jamb, seam-bustin' full of lambs sacrificed to the Lord God Almighty. Scripture just runs with the mortal gorm of the sacrificial lamb."

"They ain't atalkin' about my lamb, Granny. The Lord God ain't askin' for my one little black buck sheep."

"Took the widow's mite, didn't he?"

"He kin have my thirteen pennies," the boy said, weeping silently now.

"Oh, Jerry, Jerry," the old woman cried, "it's on account of I want you to walk in the paths of righteousness, for His Name's Sake. I got my reasons, and they ain't selfish reasons, neither. You listenin', boy?"

No answer.

"I am like Abraham whom the Lord commanded to sacrifice his only son. And when the fire was laid and the boy bound, an Angel of the Lord called unto him out of heaven staying his hand. And behold, behind him was a ram caught in a thicket by the horns. Do you understand me, Jeremiah?"

No answer.

"Musta fallen asleep. Reckon it's hard for a young'un to understand, even if sacrificin' the ram *did* save a beloved son."

But Jeremiah was not asleep. While Samantha was retelling the story of Abraham and Isaac he was slipping from the loft window, feeling with his bare toes for the well-known toe holds. He had dressed with utmost stealth and had even thought to put a tallow candle and matches in his pocket. The old wisteria vine offered friendly support as he came breathlessly, silently, down the side of the cabin.

He dropped to his feet as easily as a cat, and stood for a moment listening to Granny's voice, the whisper of the fly shuttle, and the thud of the treadle. It was a night of great moths, fluttering velvet-winged against the lighted windowpanes—lost souls speaking of rust and corruption to Samantha Kincaid, although Lilith Tarleton could once have named the tawny Cecropia and moon-marked apple-green Luna whispering against the glass. A little screech owl quavered his repetitious

71

question from deep in the Tarleton woods, and a distant hound began to bay at the new sickle moon, answered by some other plumb miserable dog on a remote farm across the valley.

Had not David himself, fleeing from Saul and from the King of Gath, escaped to the cave of Adullam? And who would think to look in the Tarleton cave up Bean Blossom Creek for a boy and his mortally endangered lamb?

Determination flowed into Jeremiah's lungs with the cool night air as he shuffled his bare feet in the icy dew to keep them warm. The sky was a deep blue earthenware crock of stars cupping the fragrant mid-summer night. The creek snaked up the hollow like quicksilver in the creases of your hand, and the far woods were a mortal mystery of cavernous shadow.

As Jeremiah pussyfooted toward the barn, he glanced back just once at the comfortable lamplight streaming from the cabin windows. Then, squaring his shoulders, he padded down the footworn path to the stable. He needed no light to find Danny's new lead rope, nor the lamb himself. A faint ray from some friendly star fell through the window upon the gentle creature breathing evenly as he lay curled in deep, clean straw. Jerry went to him quickly, but the lamb did not start up in fright, stiff-legged and tense, as he might have done if awakened in the night by a stranger. He bleated a soft welcome and nuzzled Jerry's hand.

"They won't never slaughter you, Danny," he whispered, "lessen they slaughter me first. We're agoin' to run away and live in a cave, and they ain't never agoin' to find us."

It would be fearsome and strange to hide on Lafe Tarleton's place after all the stories Granny had told Jeremiah.

The cool, solid voice of Uncle Hiram was remembered in his ears denying that anywhere on earth were there witches or specter hounds or haunts. But by faint moonlight such reasoning was hard to recapture. Was there not ghostly violin music from his dead mother's own fiddle? The shrill neighing of Josiah Tarleton's great black racing stallion dead this quarter century? What of the wandering souls some folks called moths which Lilith Tarleton had caught with a long-handled net in the dusk and pinned till Judgment Day in cases lined with black velvet? What of the birdcalls that were not birdcalls, which on a quiet evening still echoed down the valley? Not even Uncle Hiram denied that Lilith Tarleton had been buried in a coffin hollowed from a green poplar log (that shortly after sent a shoot to the sunshine and now was feasting its roots upon her moldering corpse).

Oh, it was fair witchy no matter what Uncle Hiram said, to think of Lafe Tarleton whose tongue was split like a devil's hoof from birth; who made strange noises with his mouth but could not utter a human word. No wonder folks preferred to use the Saunders Mill on Blue Lick River. It came to the boy with a sense of shock that if Lafe was his mam's brother, he must be Jeremiah's uncle.

"Man or devil," said Jeremiah softly, "Uncle Lafe ain't as dangerous as Mr. Turner. We're agoin' to the Tarleton cave, Danny, jest like I said."

Jerry came to the creek and stood for a moment thinking how best to hide any trace that Danny and he had come this way. Then as instinctively as a young fox tricks the hounds without any lessons from a wise old vixen, Jerry bethought him that running water would cover any footprint or scent. They would wade the half mile to the cave, trusting that none of the pools were too deep at this time of year and that the ghost of Lilith would not rise from its poplar coffin to open the floodgates upon them.

At first the lamb reared and bleated when drawn into the shallow stream. Later, shivering and miserable but somehow soothed by Jeremiah's encouraging voice and affectionate hand, he followed the boy up the stream. Low-hanging willows brushed their faces. A drowsing bittern leapt from the reedy margin with a startled croak. Once, rounding a bend, they heard the half-human whimpering of baby raccoons following the

73

mother in search of crayfish. Lamb and boy stood motionless and silent watching the plump ringtailed creatures, shadowy in the faint moonlight, working industriously through the shallow water with their sensitive hands. Then a splash made by the restless lamb sent the whole family scurrying for safety. Deep in the Tarleton woods a whippoorwill began his lonely serenade.

"Seems like we've come a far piece," Jeremiah said, "and we ain't even reached the Tarleton fence. Don't rightly recollect that willow tree yonder."

You had to have faith and eyes like a cat to travel safely through the immense, mysterious world of night. The homely and familiar landmarks of the pasture were twisted and lengthened by shadows. Dips between little hills became bottomless pools of dusk, while the larger hills loomed like mountains toward the incredibly distant, high horizons. But the friendly fiddling of the cicadas and tree toads and peepers was comforting.

"Leastways we got our ownselves," Jerry said. "I might be afeared if you wasn't with me, Danny."

At the rail fence dividing the Kincaid pasture from the forbidden Tarleton wilderness Jeremiah looked back where Granny's light showed warm and comforting far down-hollow, and a feeling of unutterable loneliness came over him.

"Cain't turn back now," he whispered to his lamb; "cowardy-calves don't get nowhar in this world. This ain't half as dangerous as Mr. Turner's slaughterhouse."

Thinking again of that time he had watched a slaughtering on a frosty November morning—the pigs squealing wildly, the great sledge hammer descending on their skulls before they were yanked aloft by hooks and chains to be bled; the gentle lambs being driven bleating to the knife; the fires like those of hell itself roaring under the great iron kettles of water—forcing himself to remember that scene, he realized that specter hounds and haunts were indeed small danger compared to what awaited Danny on the morrow if they returned to the cabin.

More determined than ever, he ducked under the

fence where it crossed the stream, pulling the lamb after him, and plunged up the ever-narrowing ravine through the gloom of overhanging trees.

Only once before in his life, and then by daylight, had he explored this rocky gorge as far as the entrance to the cave below the mill. The water was swift here and the ledges of limestone over which it tumbled were slippery underfoot. His feet went ever more slowly over this uncertain and unknown creek bottom.

"We ain't afeared, are we?" Jeremiah whispered.

The lamb began to bleat sadly.

"Hush, Danny. Lafe's agoin' to hear you."

At last the old stone mill came into view, standing massive and dark in the starlight. The slates gleamed dully on the roof and water dripped from the ancient silent wheel. A narrow sheet of silver water slipped over the mossy dam, making a liquid music in the vast silence. Jeremiah half expected to see dim lights moving about in the mill. It would not have surprised him if the wheel had begun to turn, grinding some ghostly grist for men long dead and buried. But wheel and stones were still; no human of this world or spirit of the next was there to lift the gate in the flume to start the water of the head race cascading over the wheel.

Above them, and hidden from the mill, yawned the dark entrance of the little cave. Trying to keep the pebbles from rattling beneath their feet, they climbed to the haven Jeremiah was seeking. Vines of bittersweet and honeysuckle fringed the opening in the rocks from which came the cool, dank odor of moss and fungus. If John the Baptist had lived on locusts and wild honey, Jerry figured *he* could. Luscious dewberries were in season, and he could get fish from the stream; at night he could take the lamb out to graze. It was a wonderful place to hide.

But Jerry's hands were shaking as he lit his tallow candle, and the zigzag flight of a frightened bat gave him a start as the candlelight explored the vaulted roof above them. It was smaller than he imagined it would be, going less than twenty feet under the ledge, but it

75

would make them a fine home. Luckily most of the cave was dry, and a great drift of last year's oak leaves could be their bed.

Jeremiah felt they were like birds escaped from the snare of the fowlers as mentioned in the Scriptures; they were foxes that had gone to ground far from the cry of the pack. He said a quick "thank you kindly" to his Maker for bringing them safely to this cave.

And then they heard it plainly, unmistakably—the music of the ghostly violin coming from the direction of the mill. And Jeremiah said it was as though a spirit passed before his face; and the hair of his flesh stood up. A moment later boy and lamb were racing madly down the creek bed, stumbling over rocks, slipping on mossy shelves of limestone. For a few moments the forgotten candle guttered in the wind. Then it went out. And they were in terrifying darkness, fleeing for their lives from the music of the ever-more-eerie violin.

At last they were safe in the Kincaid pasture, but they did not stop until they came, wet and exhausted, to Danny's stall in the barn, there to lie panting and trembling in the straw.

"That were my mam," Jeremiah whispered; "you heered her playing her fiddle. She's dead and buried in her bury hole, but she's afiddlin' up there by the Tarleton mill. It were a sign, Danny. She come back to warn us."

Jeremiah thought that in a few minutes, when he got rested, he would creep back to the cabin and climb through the window into his loft room. But he fell asleep out of sheer weariness with his arm around his lamb.

And there, after a wild search with her lantern, Granny found them. Holding up the light, she looked down upon the soaked and tattered pair, seeing them through unaccustomed tears. Shaking her head slowly from side to side, she said, "What's a body gonna do?"

7 SARPINT AND APPLE

Sometimes life in Cat Hollow would laze along for days, easy-going as a chicken hawk soaring in circles above the valley. Then, swiftly, as that same hawk could pounce on a bobwhite, a moment would arrive when everything was fuss and feathers.

Granny Kincaid had been laboring night and day on "Cat Hollow Wedding," singing mysterious verses to herself as she "inlaid" sprightly figures of colored wool:

> "The fair young maid with golden hair
> Bewitched him like a demon;
> She took him far from his mother's care
> (That traipsin' fiddlin' woman).
>
> "The infare held at the bridegroom's home
> Were a frolic fair to see;
> But the infare held at the bridegroom's home,
> Hit were the death of me. . . ."

Then one morning before sunup, on the very day Hiram was coming to build the fence, Samantha jumped out of bed, saying, "Land of Goodness, Jeremiah. I been aworkin' so hard on that kiver I clean forgot my jams and jellies."

Granny prided herself upon being the "consarvin'est" woman in Fulton Township. Her barberry preserves seemed to challenge the rhetorical question in Matthew 7:16: "Do men gather grapes of thorns, or figs of thistles?" Samantha could even make the thorny wild gooseberry harmonize with apple juice, orange rind, and sugar to perfect a concoction which Uncle Hiram averred was the nearest thing to heaven this side of harp music. And her spiced elderberries (spread thick with home-churned butter on home-baked bread) always tasted like more to Jerry Kincaid.

Each year Samantha put up whole masonry crocks of apple butter cooked in day-old cider; quart upon quart of spiced cherries with vinegar, sugar, whole cloves, and stick cinnamon; red currant jam; wildcherry jam; wild-grape jelly, and peach preserves. She never begrudged the all-too-scanty egg money that purchased lemons and almonds for her rhubarb marmalade.

Today red raspberries were ripe. And Jeremiah was more than willing to scrabble through the brambles with a milk pail in gratitude for Granny's great concession to let him keep the lamb until autumn. A handful for the pail, then a handful for his ownself—pleasant enough punishment for having run away in the night. Jerry would have stayed with the job for hours, but here came Hiram and Tildy in the jolt wagon.

Fence-building and preserving, all on the same day. Jerry figured he'd be running back and forth from lamb pen to berry patch till he was well-nigh tuckered. But Granny decreed, to Jeremiah's delight, that menfolks should do men's work and womenfolks should do women's.

"I'm agoin' to learn this girl-child how to make preserves," Samantha explained; "now run along, Jerry, and help Uncle Hiram."

It was a proud moment when Jeremiah took his end

of the crosscut saw down in the locust grove. Soon the first post was cut and peeled and lay shining, honey-yellow in the sun.

"Locust posts," said Uncle Hiram, relighting his pipe, "is the lastin'est posts you can put in the ground; hard as iron and jest about as heavy."

"Ary a critter can get through the fence we're agoin' to build."

"Sink the posts so deep and nail the boards so close," Uncle Hiram promised, "no animal in Pike County could scramble under or clamber over."

"Reckon it'll pleasure Granny?"

"Not extra-special," Hiram said, puffing thoughtfully; "jest tolerable."

"But iffen it keeps Danny out of mischief?"

"Jerry, there's bigger matters in this world than you can see through the knothole in a board fence."

"I don't rightly understand yore meaning, Uncle Hiram."

"Wal, it's kind of hard to explain, Jerry. Granny suspicions that lamb same reason she suspicions anything Tarleton. Fence'll hold the lamb, all right, but it won't hold the boy."

"I won't ever run away again," Jerry promised.

"It ain't just arunnin' away in the flesh," Hiram said, puckering his forehead. "It's arunnin' away in the spirit Granny's afeared of."

"Now yo're riddlin' me a riddle, Uncle Hiram."

"S'pose I gotta begin 'way back at the beginnin'," Hiram said, placing the saw for another cut. "You ain't never agoin' to understand that 'Cat Hollow Wedding' kiver if I don't tell you about the Tarletons."

Josiah Tarleton, Hiram told the boy, was everything Samantha's David wasn't: he was big and dark, while David was middling-sized and sandy-haired; he was tolerably rich, while David was church-mouse poor. Samantha and David were so honest they wouldn't steal a pin; Josiah was a horse trader and a gambling man—always cutting off for the Kentucky bluegrass to race his big black stallion (great-grandpappy of Lafe's present stud). It was down in the bluegrass that Josiah met Lilith Henderson, married her on the rebound, you might say, just to spite his true love Samantha.

"True love don't never come out right in the song ballads," Jeremiah observed. "Mostly both lovers die; and a white rose grows from her grave and a red rose from his'n."

"Life is maughty like song ballads sometimes," Uncle Hiram agreed, refilling his pipe. "Lilith's pap was fit to be tied when she run off with Josiah Tarleton—same as in every ballad you ever heered sung."

He hadn't come galloping after the bride and groom, but he hadn't forgiven them, either; and Lilith had mourned it to the day she was buried in the poplar log.

"Why were she buried in sech a witchy kind of coffin, Uncle Hiram?"

"Nothin' peculiar about it at all," Hiram explained, "but it jest about proved to most folks that Lilith *were* a witch. It's agettin' ahead of my story. But since you asked me spang-out I'll tell you jest what happened. Now keep up your end on that saw, son."

Lilith was an educated woman and a pretty one. So naturally no one in Cat Hollow or Fulton Corners had really trusted her. Furthermore, she was an outlander from the great city of Louisville. As if this were not enough she didn't call birds just "Peter-peter" birds and "sugar-water" birds and "yellow-hammers" and the like. She had fancy names for every last one, just like she had fancy names for the plants she found in the woods and the moths she caught with her net. She didn't do her washing on Monday, her ironing on Tuesday, and her baking on Saturday the way any honest, God-fearing, Christian woman would. Like as not she'd be bringing in a lady-slipper flower from the woods to plant in a window box, or trying to find where a hummingbird had its nest (like a knot on a bough, no bigger than a silver quarter).

"But why were she buried in a poplar log?"

"I'm acomin' to it," Hiram said, sitting on a stump to take a breather.

A favorite poplar tree just outside her bedroom window had been blown down in a storm. Arabella was thirteen that year and Lafe a surly, voiceless, rabbit-shy moon child of eleven. Lilith was ailing and couldn't get out to see the flowers she loved. She bethought her that she would like a seven-foot length of the big poplar log hollowed out for a window box beneath her bedroom window. Since she was ill, Josiah Tarleton had granted her whim and called in Hiram to gouge the green wood from the bole. But no flowers had ever been planted in that log, unless you could call Lilith a flower.

"Maybe she were a trifle out of her mind those last mortal days of her life," Hiram said sadly, "and then again maybe she weren't. Leastways, who could deny her sech a simple wish as to be buried in that log? Made a maughty purty coffin all fitted up with a slab cover, if I do say it."

"And it were fair creepy how the log sent up a poplar shoot, weren't it, Uncle Hiram?"

"Most natural thing in the world," Uncle Hiram said; "poplar and willow'll often do that. Seen willow fence posts sprout leaves many a time. Things folks call witchy is jest things folks don't understand. Wal, we gotter get back to work, Jeremiah, if we're agoin' to build that fence."

So Hiram never did get around that day to Jerry's mother Arabella, trained to play the fiddle, or the "Cat Hollow Wedding" that joined her to Samantha's only son, Seth. And when Jeremiah spoke of the ghostly fiddle music that had frightened him from the cave even Uncle Hiram was puzzled and disturbed.

"Don't reckon there's any sech thing as a haunt," he said doubtfully, "but fiddle music, comin' from nowhar—it do seem mighty peculiar."

For an hour or two they worked more and talked less. They hitched up Andrew Jackson to the stone boat to pull their posts to the site of the new pen. And Jerry became so excited about their work, and about his lamb, that he forgot all about the other questions he had intended to ask about his mother. He was figuring now some method by which he could keep his lamb not only until next autumn, but all the days of Danny's life. There seemed to be only one solution. If Danny could take a blue ribbon at the County Fair he would never be sold to Mr. Turner. He thought about it all the time he was digging postholes and all the time they were tamping in the sturdy posts. Once, when he and Hiram were resting for a moment in the cool, half dark of Danny's stall in the barn, Jerry questioned:

"When you afiggerin' to ask Granny?"

" 'Bout what?"

" 'Bout goin' to the fair, of course."

"Directly, I reckon."

"Right this minute?"

"Suppertime's soon enough."

"I'm that beholden," Jerry said joyously, "I could hug you, Uncle Hiram."

"Better wait and see if we kin get around her," Hiram said. "I've schemed me a scheme. But your granny's agoin' to twist and squirm like a weasel in a poke."

"You can wrop her 'round your finger like a white-oak splint."

"I used to brag that brag," Hiram admitted, "but lately I ain't so certain."

"I sure hope you can," said Jeremiah, " 'cause Danny and me got our hearts set on the blue ribbon and the cash prize."

"A heart set is a heart broken," Hiram warned, then looking at the broad back, square frame, and deep fleece of the lamb, he added a note of hope: "He's sure got the makin's, Jeremiah."

It was pleasant there in the dusk-dark eating by first lamp-light on the blue gingham tablecloth laid with willow ware plates and bone-handled cutlery. Boy and man had come in weary, begrimed and happy from building the fence. They had washed in cistern water from the pump at the sink, dried themselves on the roller towel and run a comb through tousled locks. Now, after the brief blessing, thanking the Lord God Almighty for their victuals, they were wading into the side meat and cornbread.

When the menfolk's plates were heaped with viands, Samantha and Mathilda could take their places at the table—making talk about whether the raspberry would jell properly, and offering samples of their day's preserving. It seemed a likely moment to tackle Granny Kincaid, who was already thanking Hiram for the fence.

"It's real neighborly and Christian of you, Hiram. Now when you and Tildy go home tonight I want you should both take some raspberry jelly. Little enough, the way you've both been working."

Yes, it seemed like the perfect moment to pop the question, but Hiram was biding his time like a cat watching a mousehole. He praised Samantha for her scrumptious jelly, and he asked her how her "Cat Hollow Wedding" counterpane was progressing. He said her apple pie was "purty near good enough to eat."

Jerry knew very well what Hiram was planning. He was only afeared that too much sweetening might spoil the batter. It was his own idea to offer to wash dishes if Tildy would wipe, which should have revealed that something was brewing—two young'uns offering to do dishes without being asked.

After the table had been cleared Samantha sat in her rocking chair humming "Billy Boy," her toe just touching to accentuate the beat, the rockers creaking out the rhythm. Uncle Hiram was well aware that you could judge Samantha's mood to a nicety by watching the pace of her rocking chair which could canter, trot, rack, single-foot, and walk; could express sharp anger, uninhibited joy, or pressing sorrow; dreams of the past or hope for the future.

Just now her rocking chair proclaimed that Samantha was as sweet-tempered as church bells on a Sabbath morning, as mellow as the lamplight at her feet.

Hiram ran a few chords on his guitar, sang a phrase or two of "Billy Boy." Gay ballads or church hymns— fast jog trot or slow, easy lope—Samantha's rocking

83

chair kept the time. Hiram was watching every move Granny made out of the corner of his eye, judging the tone and timbre of her voice, still reckoning his time. When she'd sung herself out on "Rock of Ages" and "Shall We Gather at the River" he tickled her fancy with "The Sow Took the Measles and Died in the Spring."

Then, imitating a steam calliope with his mouth and running a series of glissandi on the strings of his guitar, he began "Over the Waves."

"Memorize that song, Samantha?"

"It's unbeknownst to me."

"Play it on merry-go-rounds."

Jeremiah gave Tildy a quick joyful glance.

"At county fairs," Hiram added.

There was a moment of silence in which Samantha brought her chair to a full stop. Then, catching the implication of Hiram's trickery, she started rocking like Judgment Day, her foot striking the floor with angry determination.

"No," she said; "no, we ain't agoin'."

"Ain't agoin' whar?" Hiram asked, feigning utter innocence.

"You know whar we ain't agoin'. To the County Fair, that's whar."

"Aw, Granny," Jerry protested. "I got my heart set."

"Please, Granny Kincaid," Tildy whispered.

"No," said Granny, her rocking more determined than ever. "Now stop yore tarnal pesterin'."

"But, Granny," Jerry pleaded, "I ain't never rode on the train in all my born days. We kin sit on them fancy green plush seats and watch the world go by."

"And get our silly necks broke when the cars go off the track. Oh, I might have knowed there was somethin' up; Hiram and his sweet talk, and you young'uns washin' dishes without me takin' a stick to you."

"Shucks, Granny, trains don't go off the tracks," Jerry said. "Lots of people ride the cars."

"I ain't no traipsin' woman," said Granny Kincaid, rocking pridefully, "arunnin' around the country to circuses and fairs. We had enough traipsin' fiddlin'

women in Cat Hollow, without mentioning no names."
She closed her lips tightly and gave Hiram a meaningful look which summed up a lifetime of disapproval
for Arabella; the proud bitterness of an old woman who
in forty-four years had scarcely left her hollow; the
philosophy of one who made a necessity into an abiding
virtue; who long ago had identified wandering human-
folk with wandering conscience.

"Course you ain't a traipsin' woman, Samantha,"
Uncle Hiram said soothingly, playing gentle, depreca-
tory chords on his guitar, "Nobody ever said you were
a flighty flibbertigibbet."

"But everybody goes to county fairs," Jeremiah said
wistfully.

"Not everybody," said Samantha, tapping her foot
sharply; "not old Granny Kincaid who lives on Bean
Blossom Creek."

"But, Granny, suppose my lamb won the blue ribbon
and the cash award."

"Supposing it rained lemonade," said Granny.

"He's got the makings. Uncle Hiram said so."

"That critter!" Granny scoffed, rocking a little more
gently. "You mean that pore little smidgin of lampblack? Besides, we'd have him around till Gabriel blew
his horn iffen he ever took a blue ribbon."

"Best lamb in Pike County, ain't he, Uncle Hiram?"

"Wal," said Uncle Hiram, pulling thoughtfully on
his corncob pipe, and giving Jerry a long, slow wink,
"that lamb's tolerable, jest tolerable. But if you want
blue ribbons, how about them quilts and counterpanes?"

"My kivers?" asked Samantha, stopping her rocking
chair dead in its tracks. "You mean my hand-wove
bedding?"

"Nothin' like 'em in southern Indiana," said Uncle
Hiram judiciously. "It's as certain as the life everlastin'
they'd win ribbons and a bag of cash money."

Jerry and Tildy were between laughter and tears,
they were so happy to see Uncle Hiram wrapping
Granny around his finger, but they held in, fit to burst,
fearing she'd see the trap.

"Land of Goshen," said Granny, "it just naturally

85

never entered my head to show my weavin' at a county fair." She was suddenly aware of a craving hunger she had never before admitted: to be admired and praised even by outlanders for her handiwork; to show the world the product of her loom.

"Maybe some folks got more book-larnin' than Granny," said Uncle Hiram, purring like a tomcat stealing Jersey cream, "maybe some womenfolks got bigger high-heeled notions. But when it comes to making kivers"—he shook his head to emphasize his profound admiration—"there ain't a weaver in the state of Indiana can hold a candle to her."

"If I do say it myself, who shouldn't," Granny apologized boastfully, "I've made me some real nice quilts and counterpanes in my day."

"Nice?" said Uncle Hiram, grinning at the children. "Them covers is purty as the first leetle redbud along the blossom bough. Outland women'll be green-eyed, they'll be so jealous." He pulled with deep contentment on his corncob pipe.

Samantha was now rocking with slow, dreamy strokes, her old rocking chair making a pleasant, fiddle-like creaking in the lamplit room. She was busy counting her prize possessions on her well-worn fingers, visualizing the handsome patterns all hung for display. She was proud as Solomon of her "Rose of Sharon," her "Chips and Whetstones," and her "Tennessee Trouble." On the other hand, she hated to leave behind such time-tested favorites as her "Cat Track and Snail Trail" and "Soldiers' Return." Then she was struck by a real inspiration. She would finish her "Cat Hollow Wedding" for the Pike County Fair—there wouldn't be another counterpane like it in all creation.

Granny's cheeks began to glow the poppy-petal pink she sometimes dyed her wool. Her eyes were as bright as the wishing star just risen above the horizon, and her heart fluttered like a sugar-water bird held prisoned in the hand. You could tell by the way she rocked that she hadn't even suspicioned Uncle Hiram of playing a trick upon her—whetting her pride and coaxing her vanity.

"You figger my new counterpane . . .?" Granny began.

"Jest the thing," Hiram hastened to agree; "seems like you've wove horses racin' and a woman fiddlin'. Jest the sort of kiver to take the blue ribbon at a county fair."

Samantha's chair stopped with ominous abruptness. Fiddling women! Horse racing! Gambling! What could she be thinking of, taking Jeremiah to such a place as the fair? The cover itself was a sermon against such sin.

"Hiram Douglas," she cried, "yore the sarpint in the Garden of Eden, offerin' me the apple. I said 'No' and I mean 'No.' We ain't agoin' to the fair."

"But, Granny, you said. . ." Jeremiah began.

"Didn't say any sech thing." Oh, she wanted to go as passionately as either of the children. But remembering how Arabella had lured Seth into just such vanities, she steeled herself to be strong for Kincaids of all generations. Was it the Tarleton in Jeremiah that made him so restless, made him ache to go outland where he would see handsome horses racing and talk to wicked outlanders rich with silver money? City folks were as little to be trusted as Babylonians in the Bible (or Philistines or Moabites). Outland was a fearsome, unknown place of painted Jezebels, winebibbers, and heathen unbelievers. Just a moment ago she had been thinking how she would pack her quilts for shipping, and how they would even take Jeremiah's black lamb, if Old 99 would tote him in the baggage coach ahead.

Now with a lump in her throat and an ache in her heart she was saying fiercely, "We're not agoin'. We ain't ever agoin' to ary fair; and no back talk, Jeremiah."

Uncle Hiram would have given up the fight. But seeing the woebegone faces of Jerry and Tildy, he rallied for one last effort. Beginning slowly, then playing with increasing tempo, he fingered the chords of "Sourwood Mountain."

"I'll never get to wear my fair-going dress," Tildy mourned. "Mamma's making it out of voile with a taffeta sash and eyelet embroidery. It's awful purty."

87

"Jeremiah," said Granny sternly, "did you tell Mathilda we was agoin' to the fair?"

"Wal, you see, Granny. . ."

"Oh, I see plain as day— thought you'd get around me. And now you've broke this girl-child's heart."

"Chickens acrowin' on Sourwood Mountain,
Hay did-dy ump did-dy id-dy um day."

sang Hiram, adding, "It were jest an idea, Samantha; shouldn't have brought it up in the first place." (He ran an ascending glissando on the guitar.) "When folks get old, it's better for 'em to set by the fire, atakin' their ease and nursin' their rheumatism."

Granny stopped rocking. "Meanin' me?"

"Might as well face it," Hiram taunted. "You ain't so young and spry as you once was, Granny."

"I'll live to dance on yore grave, Hiram Douglas, and it'll pleasure me."

" 'Fraid your fair-goin' and dancin' days are over, Samantha."

Granny sprang to her feet, her eyes bright and wicked as those of a mink in a trap. She was mad clear through and fit to be tied.

"I kin dance you down six-ways-for-Sunday!" Granny cried. "I kin sashay the livin' daylights out of you. Git up and take yore medicine like a man."

"Now remember them six chords I learned you," Hiram said, handing his guitar to Jeremiah.

There was no doubt about it. Hiram had sown the wind and he was reaping the whirlwind. He and Samantha had been aching for a showdown and the time had come. Never again in this life was Jeremiah to see so strange a dance as the one which now began with Hiram singing the verses, Jerry trying to play the chords, and Granny calling the numbers.

Wary as a pair of bantam roosters and as full of fight, they went into the ring with feathers flying. They circled left, they circled right, they swung their partners, and they promenaded as though the room were

88

somehow filled with twenty ghostly couples out of the long ago.

> "Wash your dishes, wipe them dry,
> Your true love is passing by ..."

Back in the Cumberland, when Samantha was a girl, such dances lasted all night long by the light of bayberry candles and the music of the fiddle. Now all the steps came back to her, and her young strength with them. She called the intricate numbers of "Box the Gnat," "Chase the Squirrel," and "Roll up the Ball of Yarn." In a sweet, clear, angry voice she challenged Hiram and the years. Her hands no longer seemed gnarled as she spread her skirt to curtsy low, and the gray-sprigged percale might have been a gown of silver. Oh, Hiram started out bravely enough, following the steps as best he could, but Samantha was a willow tree in Laurel Gap; a red-tailed hawk on a summer breeze. She was dancing with spirits of the departed—angrily with Josiah Tarleton; big-eyed with David Kincaid. Who could have guessed that so much energy remained in the work-worn, weather-beaten woman?

> "Eat the meat, gnaw the bone,
> Grab yore honey and go home."

Jeremiah and Tildy were between laughter and tears to see the wild, uneven contest. Big Uncle Hiram was puffing like an old horse with the heaves, but more and more gayly danced Samantha Kincaid—"Money Musk" and "Morning Star"; waltz and polka and "Soldier's Joy"; "Portland Fancy" and "Pop Goes the Weasel."

"I'll dance you right into your coffin, Hiram Douglas."

"That's sassy talk for a granny woman," Hiram panted.

"Play 'Cricket in the Frying Pan,' Jerry."

Toward the end the children could no longer stand aside. They joined the frolic, whirling and capering, gyrating and cutting pigeonwings in complete disregard of all the numbers. They squealed with laughter and shouted encouragement to Uncle Hiram, who hung on grim and determined with Granny dancing him down.

" 'Fire in the Briar Patch!' " Granny shouted.

"No!" Hiram cried. "You're killin' me, Samantha."

"Say quits?"

"I'm clean, plumb tuckered," Hiram admitted, lying back on the floor, gasping for breath and shouting with laughter.

"Take it back?" Granny leaned over Hiram still full of fight and frolic while the beaten man waved her away feebly with both hands.

"Get on yore feet and dance, Hiram Douglas."

"Can't dance another lick, Samantha."

"Too old to dance, too old to go to the County Fair? You eat them words and eat 'em proper."

"You're as spry as a gray squirrel, Granny," said Uncle Hiram, wiping his eyes with his red bandanna. "Pert as a chickadee. You're a wicked old woman and you wore me to a frazzle."

"Licked you fair and square, didn't I?" Granny said.

"Reckon you could outdance any old man at the County Fair," Hiram admitted, winking broadly at the children.

"Wal," said Samantha, weakening ever so slightly.

"Oh, we're going, we're going," the children cried, dancing in circles.

"We'll ride on the merry-go-round and the Ferris wheel and everything," Tildy shouted happily.

Hiram was still wheezing from his ordeal but he began to sing "Putting on the Agony, Putting on the Style," a fallen warrior but not a vanquished one:

"*Country lads and lasses going to the scene,*
  Looking fresh as dewdrops on the garden green;
  Crackerjack and candy eating all the while,
  Going to the circus, putting on the style."

Samantha looked tenderly but soberly from one to another of the happy faces, shaking her head sadly.

"And when Danny wins the blue ribbon. . ."

Granny put her hand on Jeremiah's shoulder to

steady him. "Now hold yore horses, Jerry. I didn't promise."

The room was suddenly so quiet you could hear the clock ticking.

"Costs a heap of cash money to go to the fair."

Granny Kincaid had followed literally the advice in St. Matthew: "Lay not up for yourselves treasures upon earth, where moth and rust doth corrupt, and where thieves break through and steal: But lay up for yourselves treasures in heaven . . . for where your treasure is, there will your heart be also."

She had once told Jeremiah that you could put all her money in a goose quill and blow it in a chigger's eye. What little she possessed was hidden in a painted tin box under a stone of the hearth. And she did not hesitate now to unearth it before these friendly eyes and pour the nickels and dimes and copper pennies into her lap, adding up the total. She shook her head over the result, asking sadly:

"What we goin' to use for cash money, Jeremiah? Buttons?"

"Don't you worry about money, Granny."

"Cain't buy railroad tickets with moonbeams."

"I kin get a job of work somewhars," Jeremiah said proudly. "I'm the man of the family."

And although Uncle Hiram was proud to hear him say it and did not wish to tarnish this grown-up moment, he knew that Samantha would be thankful for a more practical solution. He did not wish to lose the advantage of the long evening's conniving.

"Now iffen you ain't too stiff-starch proud . . ." Uncle Hiram began.

"You mean the borrow of a loan?" asked Samantha, bridling.

"You'd have to pay back every penny, maybe with interest," Hiram hastened to say.

"Course I'm stiff-starch proud," Samantha said, "and sassy poor. I maught starve, but I'd never beg."

"But, Granny. . ." Hiram began to protest.

"Never borrowed a loan in my life. Always paid my own way and beholden to no one."

91

"But Granny! Iffen the lamb wins the cash award. . ." Jerry suggested.

"Kincaids don't spend money they ain't got."

"But I'll earn the money. Please, Granny."

"Best to forget the whole thing," said Granny, her firm upper lip trembling ever so slightly. "County fairs is sinful and extravagant. Never did nobody any good."

"We could pray for money," Jerry said, grasping at straws. "We could ask the Lord God Almighty for jest a leetle cash money."

"Not in this house," said Samantha. "Things of the spirit, yes. Things of the flesh, no. I reckon the Almighty is plumb disgusted to hear what most folks pray for."

"Come, Tildy," Uncle Hiram said. "Time we was gettin' you back to your maw. You're much too big to cry." Taking his guitar under his arm, Hiram started for the door as Jeremiah gave him a look of pure misery.

"Don't forget to take your raspberry jelly," Samantha said. "And thank you kindly for the fence."

" 'Tween't nothing," Hiram belittled, closing the door softly behind him. But if Samantha could have seen his face she would have known that this time he wasn't taking "No" for an answer.

8 SASSAFRAS AND WILD HONEY

The dream of Saturday night was as real as any
story or poem in his *McGuffey's Reader*. And the
burlap poke of sassafras roots sinfully harvested on the
Sabbath was proof positive that dreams could come
true. Now, feeding his lamb before starting to the
Corners with his first pay load, he was still at a loss
to explain his good fortune.

"I heered a ruckus in the foreyard," Jerry explained
to his lamb, "like folks beating pans and pails at a
shivaree. I clumb out of my window and sneaked around
the cabin and thar were a lot of people all witchy and
wan in the moonlight . . . Now eat yore mash, Danny, or
you ain't ever agoin' to grow up to be a prize lamb. . . .

"Acted real mean and ornery they did. The ruckus
they made seemed to come from a far piece; other
side of the grave most likely. Inside the cabin I could
hear fiddles just as witchy. . . . No, I ain't agoin'
to give you a bottle; high time you was weaned. . . . Now
eat yore mash or I'll whop you. . . .

"Musta made a noise or something, 'cause all of a

sudden all them haunts disappeared into thin air like a specter hound at cock's crow. Inside the house the fiddles all stopped and the candles went out . . . Don't be skeered, Danny, it were just a dream most likely. . . .

"Then right through the door that wasn't open or nothin' stepped my mam and pap just like they look in the weddin' picture Granny's got hid in her bottom drawer. Walked right spang through the closed door and out into the foreyard. . . . No, I ain't agoin' to feed you this carrot till you eat your plain victuals.

"Wal, I weren't afeared of my mam and pap, and they weren't afeared of me. They didn't say ary a word, but Pap took one hand and Mam took the other and we started by a path I don't rightly recollect—a secret path to the Tarleton place they must of used when they were courtin'. My mam were dressed like moonlight in her weddin' gown, her feet hardly teched the ground. . . .

"It weren't all clear exactly whar we was goin' or why. But I remember tellin' 'em all about you, Danny, and all the trouble I been havin' tryin' to earn a little cash money. They didn't say ary a word, but they smiled at me and toted me along between them, just like we were all three walkin' on air. . . . Oh, it were a ghosty dream, Danny . . . All right, you can have your carrot now. . . .

"I told 'em about hoein' tobacco for twenty-five cents a day at Saunders' farm, and pickin' potato bugs for a nickel a thousand. And how mean old man Saunders was; and how I was never agoin' to earn enough to get to the County Fair. So then my pap stopped beside a sassyfras tree: I could smell the spicy twigs and see the little berries and feel the rough bark—and I knew right away what he meant; it'd jest naturally never occurred to me to dig sassyfras roots for cash money. I were that beholden, Danny, I wanted to hug my mam and pap, but when I threw my arms around 'em they weren't there—nothing but moonlight and faraway fiddle music. And I woke up in my own bed and I were cryin'. . . . Ain't that a queer sort of dream? . . . Reckon I'll be able to wean you yit if I work hard

94

enough; I gotta polish yore little horns till they shine like buckeyes, and bresh yore wool till it shimmers like velvet. Yo're goin' to be the purtiest lamb that ever won a blue ribbon."

Yes, Jerry thought, it were all like a miracle in the Bible.

For the dream of Saturday night was a reality of Sunday morning. At sunup on the Sabbath, without waking his granny, he had slipped out of bed, and, armed with poke and ax, had started to search for the secret path once used by his mother and father. He went the whole length of the rail fence between the Kincaid pasture and the Tarleton woods without finding any place that seemed familiar in his dream. He was about to give up the search when through a little opening in the brush he saw not one but several sassafras trees with their little blue berries and deep-ridged trunks. For several hours he busily hacked in the ground for chunks of the aromatic roots which he put in his sack.

"My mam and pap want us to go to the fair, Danny," Jeremiah said. "It's a sure sign."

In the days preceding his dream the business about a sign from heaven had become all-important in the Kincaid cabin. While Jeremiah had racked his brains and labored long hours to make a little cash money to take them to the fair, Granny had quoted Scripture against his plans.

"The love of money is the root of all evil," Samantha said; "the Good Book's heapin' full and runnin' over with sermons agin the sins of wealth."

"That ain't all it says in the Bible," Jeremiah protested. "How about the good and faithful servant who increased his talents? How about whar it says 'Thy work shall be rewarded'?"

"If you walk in His way and keep His Commandments," Granny admitted reluctantly, "blessed shall be thy basket and store."

"I'm atryin' to walk in His way and keep His Commandments," Jeremiah said sadly, "but my basket's still empty."

"Maybe the Lord God Almighty figgers that wantin'

95

to go to a county fair ain't a righteous kind of hankerin'."

"You mean, if he *don't* let me earn the money, he *don't* want us to go?"

"That's plain as Scripture."

"Then iffen he *does* let me earn the money, he *does* want us to go?"

"Could be," Samantha puzzled. "I reckon now you put it thataway we can count on the Lord to give us a sign one way or the other."

"I'm agoin' to help him give me the right sign," Jerry promised. "I'm agoin' to work my fingers to the bone."

And so every day after milking the cow in the morning and tending to his other chores he tramped the roads of the Township hunting work. A fellow up a cherry tree wouldn't give him a job because he said young'uns ate more than they put in the pail. Man cultivating corn said he and his old nag had been hard-scrabbling those rocky acres for years—and it took more cussing and tobacco chewing than any young squirt could manage to farm his dad-gummed stump patch. Bob Peters, the station agent, pushing back his green eye-shade, said there hadn't been scarcely a telegram to deliver since McKinley was shot by that anarchist feller.

It was enough to break Jeremiah's heart the way the Lord was always on Granny's side and wouldn't give him so much as a fair-going sign. Even the thirty-five cents he made working for Old Man Saunders didn't convince Granny. And Samantha said that the dime Uncle Hiram paid him for pumping the bellows was pure charity. Jerry never should have accepted it. In fact, she made him give it back.

"Hiram's jest aidin' and abettin' yore own wayward notions," Granny said; "he's jest afiggerin' and aschemin' how to get around me. What he does ain't no sign from Heaven. . . ."

Sometimes Jerry was so discouraged he wanted to cry. He would go out to the pen and sit for an hour talking to his lamb, coddling him and petting him and feeding him carrots. Maybe he was spoiling the creature, as Granny said. It was plain ridiculous how such a big buck sheep still baaed for his bottle like a cradle baby. But at long last he was beginning to eat the cracked corn and oats and wheat bran and linseed meal on which he was being fitted. Granny begrudged the nickels which bought him feed, but she had to admit that the yoke was coming up in his fleece until he looked like a picture on a calendar.

"Iffen I can only earn some cash money," Jerry whispered to his pet. "Iffen the Lord'll only give me the go-ahead, there ain't the least doubt you'll take a blue ribbon, yo're so fat and sassy."

The lamb was interested in nothing but carrots and nuzzled incessantly at Jeremiah's pocket.

"Foursquare as a brick smokehouse," Jerry said admiringly; "strong as an ox. You got little nubbins of devil horns ashowin' through your curly head wool. And yo're wicked as your mam and pap put together; but I wouldn't trade you for a store-bought bicycle."

But what good did it do to polish the horns and hoofs and comb the fleece so clean and bright if the Almighty was aholdin' out on the fair-goin' sign? Not a dirty tag or bur or tick in Danny's wool; joyous and pert, with eyes like jewels. But who would ever know it if Jerry couldn't earn the money to go to the fair?

Meanwhile Samantha, working furiously on her new cover, was trying to tell Jeremiah why she feared the outland. It had something to do with his mother and father, that he knew. The verses Granny sang these days hinted strongly that his mam, the traipsin' fiddlin' woman, had somehow been the ruination of his pap.

> "One April day he plowed her field,
> She said, 'Now yo're my plighted.'
> An evil troth did that day yield;
> Come June they were united.
>
> "Oh, a ribbon bow to bind her hair,
> A kerchief for her weeping,
> A golden ring for her finger fair
> To shine as she lay sleeping."

97

"Course Arabella didn't have no mother you could rightly call," Samantha admitted. "Lilith were a bad mother alive and a worse one dead. That girl-child of hern used to swim in Bean Blossom Crick without wearin' a stitch. Rode horses astride and bareback like a shameless hussy. Time she was sixteen she was amakin' eyes at Seth somethin' scandalous. No wonder the hull Township shivareed us after the infare. Just like Absalom turned against David in the Bible, Seth turned agin his pap. I fault yore mam fer all the trouble."

"Sometimes I dream about my mam," Jeremiah said wistfully. "She were beautiful, weren't she?"

"Yes," Samantha admitted with a sigh, "she had hair red-gold like the sun; eyes blue as blue. But like the lilies of the field she toiled not, neither did she spin. She'd ruther race that horse of hern than make a home for Seth; gamblin', traipsin', fiddle-playin', no-good woman. I memorize the year the tree fell on her pap, Josiah! Seth and Arabella were down in the bluegrass among the fleshpots of Egypt—wouldn't even come home for the funeral . . . Sin, and the wages of sin."

"Maybe my mam and pap up in heaven could ask the Lord God Almighty to give me a sign," Jeremiah said.

"They ain't up in heaven," Samantha said sternly. "Now hush."

All this had happened before the dream of the shivaree with its magic consequences.

Now, carrying his sack of sassafras roots toward Fulton Corners, Jeremiah realized happily that his dream really was the sign for which he had prayed. Yes, even Granny was about ready to admit it. Of course he didn't know how much Pete Grundy would pay for sassafras, but at least he had found a way to increase his little horde of cash money. Granny had been so flabbergasted when he came in with the first roots that she had failed to scold him for breaking the Fourth Commandment. She had even forgiven him for nicking her best ax.

Instead, Samantha had merely looked at the begrimed and beaming face and at the small back bent

98

under its heavy load, repeating softly what Solomon had once said of David, "Yet young and tender and the work is great."

When she asked Jeremiah how he had come to think of sassafras, he told her of the curious portent of the previous evening. Granny was not in the least surprised to hear the details of that vision, for she herself had dreams of revelation. Indeed, she said that the infare and shivaree for Seth and Arabella were much as Jerry had dreamed them.

As Jeremiah sat with his granny enjoying the cool of the Sabbath evening and watching the purple martins skim out of the sky and rest in their gourd houses hanging in the sycamore tree, she sang new verses to her ballad:

> "The words were said, the ring was given!
> By candle, book, and bell,
> The match was never made in heaven
> That ended up in hell.
>
> "Oh, toll the church bell for the bride,
> And toll it for the groom;
> The path is flowery and wide
> Which leads but to the tomb.
>
> "Josiah—never at our board—
> Yet to the infare came,
> As reeling drunk as any lord,
> And quarrelsome as the same . . ."

"Did he fight with my grandpap Kincaid?"

"It were nip and tuck for a time," Samantha admitted; "might have been mortal gorm spilled at the infare. There weren't no love lost between David and Josiah."

"Did my pap stop 'em?"

"Hiram did. Gave Josiah a gourd of likker and laid him out in the corner. . . . You never seed such dancin', fiddlin', drinkin', and sparkin' in yore born days. And all the time my heart fit to break on account of losing Seth to that traipsin' fiddlin' woman. . . ."

"My mam's wedding dress were beautiful," Jerry said.

99

"Yes, it were," Samantha admitted. "How'd you know?"

"Seen it in my dream."

"Were she wearing a lace veil and leetle white slippers?"

"Yes, Granny."

"That were her," Granny sighed. "My, she were a picture."

"Who started the shivaree?"

"Lilith," said Samantha grimly.

"But she were dead and in her bury hole."

"Nothin' but a haunt could of wailed and howled like that female critter out there in the night," Granny said; "fair made yore flesh creep. . . ."

"What for did she crave to shivaree her own daughter's weddin'?"

"Hated me and mine," said Samantha. "She were mad as a hornet on account of Josiah had come to the infare. Maught be she saw him kiss my hand when he came in the door—silly old good-for-nothin' horse-racin' scalawag—drunk as a coot."

"Did Mam and Pap have a secret path through the Tarleton woods?"

Samantha eyed the boy sharply. "That were a witchy dream you had. No livin' soul in creation ever seed that path 'cept Seth and Arabella and my ownself. Cain't hardly find it myself these days—went in past a clump of sassyfras trees."

"That's the path they showed me," Jeremiah said. "It's a sure sign, ain't it, Granny? It's the Lord God Almighty agivin' me the fair-goin' sign."

"Wait and see how much cash money Pete Grundy'll pay for them roots," said Samantha evasively. "I ain't right-down positive sure any sign from yore mam come from the right place in the hereafter."

And just at that moment they had heard the ghostly violin, wild and sweet and far away up Bean Blossom Creek.

Remembering all this as he labored down the road with his heavy sack of sassafras roots, Jeremiah realized that it wasn't going to be easy to make Granny admit

100

that Heaven had sent a favorable sign unless he could somehow raise a whole pocket full of silver—more money than he had ever dreamed of. It was root-hog-or-die (for sassafras roots), hardscrabble or starve. But his hope and pride were soaring.

He met Tildy at the bridge and they rested for a time sitting on the stone abutment and swinging their bare brown legs over the water. They talked seriously of their need for fair-going money and speculated on the value of the sassafras.

"Wisht I could find a big pearl in a clam," Jerry said wistfully.

"Or catch a fish with a gold ring in its innards like in the fairy story," Tildy added.

"Or find a gold mine," they both said simultaneously.

"Needles."

"Pins."

"Triplets."

"Twins."

They hooked fingers and made their secret wishes, But each knew what the other was wishing.

In fact they usually could guess what the other was thinking, even what tune the other was singing to himself. They had a whole world of things they knew without telling each other: riddle-de-rhymes and play-game jingles and counting-out songs and snatches of ballads that seemed to float around in the hills like ancient echoes. No one that they could remember had ever taught them to sing at first lamplight.

> "Moonlight, starlight,
>   I guess the bears ain't out tonight."

Yes, their wishes had been identical.

And speaking of the County Fair, Tildy had made a wonderful discovery which she now shared. At the far end of the bridge a fair poster had been tacked to the boards. Careless of slivers, they raced through the shadowy tunnel to gaze with awe upon the gay picture of prize cows, pigs, horses—and even *sheep*.

"Notice anything about that ram?" Jerry asked.

"It's white," Tildy whispered.

"Any old sheep can be white," Jerry said.

"Remember what Uncle Hiram said?"

"When?"

"Time that nice Negro man came to town."

"I disremember."

"He said," Tildy faltered, groping for the words, "it don't matter whether you're white or black. It's— it's what color you are inside."

"Wish Hiram was agoin' to be the judge," Jeremiah said, taking up his heavy load. "I'll meet you at our secret place, Tildy."

Tildy understood. She dropped her eyes.

"You don't want Fud Grundy to see us," Tildy said, " 'cause I hit him with a stick."

"It's a far piece to walk to town and back."

"I ain't tired."

"Someday," said Jeremiah, "after I've licked Fud Grundy by my ownself I'll be proud to walk right spang through the Corners with you."

"I'll wait at our secret place," Tildy said. "I'll allus do anything you want me to all our born days."

An even more beautiful and a far larger poster adorned one whole side of the store: it showed prancing horses with ribbons in their manes; handsomely groomed and curled beef cattle with broad white faces; pigs as plump as balloons—and yes, sheep. But again these handsome, foursquare, snub-nosed fellows were glittering white. Maybe no shepherd from Dan to Beersheba had ever been foolish enough to show a black lamb at a county fair. Jerry turned away with a sigh, shifted his heavy sack to the other shoulder, and prepared to enter the store.

Fud Grundy was sitting astride the hitching rail reading "Buster Brown" in the funny paper. Jeremiah stopped to peer over his shoulder, so Fud lowered the paper and began chanting:

> "Ragpicker, ragpicker,
>   Come to town to make a dicker."

"These ain't rags," Jeremiah said. "They're sassyfras roots."

"Where'd you get 'em?"

"Bet you'd like to know."

Fud thought a moment and then began chanting again in a high nasal twang:

> "Old Jeremiah, the sassyfras man,
>   He digs sassyfras all he can."

Jeremiah briefly considered the joy of putting down his sack and knocking Fud off the hitching rail.Then he remembered that business came before pleasure. He turned on his heel and went in through the neatly repaired screen door.

As the bell tinkled Pete Grundy looked up from his checker game with Grandpa Meeker.

"Now what?" Grundy asked.

"Sassyfras roots, Mr. Grundy."

"Ain't hardly worth handlin','" the storekeeper complained. "Cain't give you more than two cents a pound."

Grundy crossed to the counter and put the bag on the scales. He balanced and rebalanced the scale arm.

"Eighteen pounds."

"Says eighteen and a half."

"Eighteen," Grundy insisted, "times two is thirty-six cents."

"Is that all?"

"Cipher it for yourself."

"I mean it's not going to be enough."

Grundy shoved the change across the counter and went back to his checker game.

"Thank you kindly," Jerry said slowly.

"What you saving up for? To go to college?"

Jeremiah didn't answer. He could hear Granny say, "Thirty-six cents. That's real good, Jeremiah, but it ain't anythin' like a fair-goin' sign from the Almighty." Thirty-six plus the thirty-five cents Mr. Saunders had paid to him made seventy-one cents. Add the thirteen he had saved previous to this summer, and it made eighty-four. He was richer than he had ever been in his life before, but it took real cash money to go to the fair.

The bell tinkled again and Archie's little freckle-faced sister, Fanny McCoy, came hippety-hopping into the store. Grundy started to rise again, exasperated at the new interruption.

"No wonder you rook me at checkers, you old buzzard. You got twice as long to figger every move." He glared at Grandpa Meeker, who grinned slyly.

"Maw wants a pint of wild honey."

Grundy shook his head and sat down again to ponder over his next move.

"Aunt Margaret's cough come back bad," Fanny explained, hopping in a circle on one foot. "Maw wants to make wild-honey cough syrup."

"Ain't had a lick of wild honey in this store since Dewey took Manila."

"Even the bees is gettin' lazier, seems like," Grandpa Meeker opined.

"Maw'll be real mad," said the freckle-faced girl hopping carefully along one crack all the way to the door; "she don't like 'No' for an answer."

Grundy moved cautiously, keeping his finger on his king. "Ask your maw if tame honey won't do."

The door slammed and the bell tinkled.

Grundy looked sharply at the boy. "Now there's an idea for you, Jeremiah."

Jerry turned and listened.

"You want to get rich quick?" the storekeeper continued. "Go out and find a wild-bee tree—pay you ten cents a pound."

Jeremiah's eyes brightened. "How do I find a wild-bee tree, Mr. Grundy?"

Grundy was concentrating on his next move. "Huh . . . why . . . just find a bee and follow it home."

"Sounds real easy," Jerry said. "Gee, thanks. Thank you kindly, Mr. Grundy." Turning on his heel, he almost ran from the store, a little rhyme forming in his mind:

> Bees
> Honey
> A bee tree
> Money.

It was an enchanting and haunting little tune. He was as happy as a bear cub with similar prospects.

"Don't care a picayune how you waste that boy's time, do you?" Grandpa Meeker said.

"What's time to a boy?"

Jeremiah found Mathilda waiting, as she had promised, between the two ancient sycamores. He did not reveal his secret for several moments, but savored it, enduring the time he might find a pollen-laden bee in a clover blossom. He told her sadly that his dream had been no fair-going sign since the sassafras had earned him only thirty-six cents. But he could not hide the note of confidence in his voice.

Soon he plucked a tickle brush of iridescent wild barley and began teasing a honeybee. The gauzy-winged insect had been laboring since sunup in a nectar-crazed frenzy of purposeful gleaning. Her delicate legs were golden with pollen as she probed with intemperate lust into the chalice of each flower. Disturbed by the wild barley broom, she circled angrily around Jeremiah's head, drawing her poisoned needle forward and under while her wings whirred high-pitched warning.

"Watch her," Jerry cried. "Watch whar she goes."

"What for?"

"Honeybee, honeybee, fly away home. Yore house is on fire and yore children will burn."

"She ain't got no home, most likely."

"Ain't ary a bee in creation," Jerry said, "don't tote her honey to her hive . . . Shucks, I lost her." He began to prod another bee with his barley straw.

"What you doin' that for?" Tildy asked.

105

" 'Cause . . . Now watch sharp."

"Well, why don't you tell me?"

"Bees, honey, a bee tree, money," Jeremiah chanted.

"Oh, Jerry, what a wonderful idea," Tildy shouted. "I jest know you thought of that, 'cause you're terrible smart."

"Ol' Pete Grundy thought of it," Jerry said truthfully. "Course we ain't found the bee tree yet."

"We will," Tildy cried. "There ain't nothin' on earth can stop us."

"Thar she goes, straight as a beeline."

"I'm acomin'," Tildy said.

"Might be a far piece," Jeremiah warned; "miles and miles most likely."

"Don't matter."

"You might git lost; you cain't keep up."

"Won't neither and kin too."

Their eyes were glued to the shimmering bee as she arrowed homeward with her golden load. Careless of rip-shin briars and rip-shank brambles they started on their quest, which was to take them up hill and down dale past springs of lonesome water (mirroring the sky) and through deep woods, fair creepy with haunts.

Their hearts were beating like moths against a lamp chimney as they crossed the pasture (sprayed with black-eyed Susans). Running with their eyes on the bee far above them, they sometimes stumbled, but were up again like young deer.

"There's another, and another!" Tildy cried.

Oh, they were on the trail, no doubt about it. The blue highroad from pasture to distant bee tree was streaked with living meteors. Now boy and girl were over a rail fence and following a clear little stream they had never explored before. The creek bottom was minty and cool under sycamores massive and dappled with light. Quails whistled from every cover, and a pair of raucous bluejays protecting their young from angry songbirds wove frantic patterns through a shadow gum tree.

Climbing now over shallow limestone ledges and following the bed of the stream toward its source, Tildy and Jeremiah were already breathing hard and wishing they might rest. It seemed the promised land must be far fields away, for suddenly the stream of water and the thin stream of bees overhead parted company. Leaving the cool creek valley, the children scrambled up a rocky pasture hill, through dewberries and cat briars, scarcely aware of scratched and bleeding legs.

They came at last to a bald dome of rock overlooking miles of checkerboarded countryside. The Kincaid cabin was hidden by a brow of the hill, but for the first time in their lives they could view complete the Tarleton house and mill and barns—the shimmering millpond above the dam and Bean Blossom Creek glinting through the trees. The wheel was so small at this great distance they might have turned it with their little fingers to grind the grist of folk as tiny as those they sometimes saw on their secret mound.

"Wisht we owned the whole shootin' match." Jeremiah sighed.

"We'd fix that little mill," Tildy said, "and we'd live in that little house, and have little cows and sheep and things."

Not just the Tarleton farm, but the whole world seemed to be theirs for the asking from that high point of rock. Blue Lick River was so small they could have dammed it with their hands; the covered bridge might have been moved upstream or down between thumb and finger. Fulton Corners was a make-believe doll town with its white church and steeple no more than three inches high and the gravestones no bigger than a fingernail.

For a few minutes they forgot all about the bees, pointing out the miniature wonders spread below them.

"I kin see yore house, Tildy."

"There's Uncle Hiram's shop and the little bitsy station."

"Thar comes Old 99."

"No bigger than a minute."

"She's ablowin' for a stop. See the steam acomin' out the whistle?"

"Cain't hear a thing."

107

"Hark a bit—you'll hear it."

Then faint and far away they heard the tinkle of the bell and whisper of the eerie whistle.

It was something Jeremiah would always remember: the tiny train pulling to a stop, the little jolt wagons dusting down the ribbony roads, and folks swarming like ants toward the station. Small but perfect colts scampered in handkerchief-sized pastures, and from the roof of a toy-sized barn white pigeons swirled like snowflakes into the sunshine.

"Granny-women, cow-brutes, ridin'-critters, and hound-dogs," Jerry said. "You could jest about cup 'em in yore two hands, seems like."

"Somebody'd sure get hurt," Tildy said seriously. "I ain't ever agoin' to do it."

"Do what?"

"Pick up people. And—and move the houses around."

Jerry laughed, and the spell was suddenly broken. "Tildy, the bees!"

"I clean forgot all about 'em."

Shading their eyes from the sun, they scanned the skies like stargazers watching for stars to wish upon. They had come far lands away—they might almost have crossed the ocean-sea. And now it would be pure misery to lose the treasure they were seeking—the bees, the bee tree, and the honey; the silver they would be paid; the chance to take their beloved black lamb to the County Fair.

A redbird was sitting in a mulberry tree treating his handsome dusty green wife to a mouth-watering feast. Everyone knows that redbirds are smart as coons. So Jeremiah asked the redbird where the bees had gone.

"Here, here, here," cried the cardinal.

"You mean right under that ol' mulberry tree?"

"Cheer, cheer, cheer," cheered the redbird, flicking his tail and stiffening his crest.

And there, certain as his name was Jeremiah, the boy discovered a bee buzzing in the trumpet of a wild columbine. Urged gently from her flower, the bee rose gleaming into the air and traced a bypath to the upper highway. Over the ridge and down she went with the children following, through long-abandoned fields of cockleburs and corn, through elderberry thicks and hazel bushes. From far below, in some lost hollow, came the clang of a distant cowbell, telling them how remote they were from any habitation.

"Are you afeared, Tildy?"

"I ain't afeared."

So they plunged down the far slope past an ancient cabin with mud-daubed chimney and sagging roof where a phoebe made her nest, through an ancient foreyard all overgrown with yellow day lilies and late roses. A hawk wheeled slowly on the rising summer air.

It was a temptation to stop and explore the cabin. But once before they had lost their bees, so they did not even open the tip-tilted door nor turn aside for apples from a laden tree. The line of bees was clearer now or they might not even have hesitated for the mother skunk, with her wide white stripes and high-curved tail, which crossed the path ahead of them (followed Indian file by six skunk kittens).

"Wisht I had one of them cute little skunk kittens," Tildy whispered.

"You kin raise 'em on bread and milk. They don't even stink."

"Boy I knew had one. Wisht I could."

"My mother'd say 'No,' I'll bet. She'd never let me."

"My granny, neither."

The skunks trundled by as serious as the Sabbath —a black-and-white procession bent on important business somewhere far down the hill.

Jerry meanwhile had kept one eye on the bees. Now that the coast was clear the boy and girl slipped swiftly down the hill through an ancient beech grove to another stream—bigger than a lick, bigger than a creek, in fact a small river.

It was so wild and remote from humankind that a wood duck had nested in a willow tree overhanging the water. They caught a bold flash of color as it whirred upstream, zigzagging through the trees.

109

There was no sign of a bridge or fallen log on which to cross. But at one place Jerry thought it was safe to wade. The smooth limestone was mossy and cool under their bare feet and the current pushed hard against their brown legs.

"Hold my hand, Jerry."

"Hold on then, scairdy."

But he was glad that they had each other's support in the swift current which might have swept them into the deep pool below the riffle.

Safely across at last, they found themselves on the edge of a vast, gloomy swamp into which the line of bees sped like silver bullets.

"We cain't go in there," Tildy whispered.

"Why cain't we?"

" 'Cause that's Dead Man's Swamp. It's full of bog-holes."

"Course it's Dead Man's Swamp. Iffen I were a bee, that's whar I'd hide my honey. Wouldn't you?"

"I reckon so, but, Jerry . . ."

"Comin' or ain't you?"

"I'm acomin'. Wait for me, Jerry."

At first they followed an old cow trail through the bog with water gleaming evilly in the ancient hoof-prints. The pools were green with algae and oily with dead swamp growth. Then the trail disappeared into heavy undergrowth, and the path of the bees took them from hummock to hummock between deep black pools. Far away a dog bayed mournfully and the distant cowbell clanged through the dark tamaracks.

Something gleamed white between the hummocks.

"What's that?" Tildy asked.

"Nothin'—jest some old bones."

"Whose bones?"

"Cow or somethin', I reckon."

"Who killed it?"

"Just died, most likely."

"How do you know?"

"Jest know," Jeremiah said. "If yo're afeared you'd better go back."

"No . . . I ain't afeared exactly."

"Bones is a good sign," Jeremiah said, " 'cause that's whar Sampson found bees and honey."

"Where'd he find 'em?"

"Carcass of a lion. Skull most likely."

A marsh bird flew up, almost from beneath their feet, uttering a harsh croaking sound. Tildy threw her arms around Jerry and held on, trembling.

"Jest an ol' bird," Jerry said.

"I'm afeared," Tildy said.

"Cain't go back now," Jerry said; "step right whar I step. I don't confidence them bogholes."

Darker and ever more forbidding the swamp closed in around them.

Again they heard the baying of a dog, this time joined by others of his lonesome breed, their voices keening for the quarry—a music full of the deepest misery in the world.

"What's that, Jerry?"

"Jest old hound-dogs."

"Wild, sheep-killin' dogs?"

"Jest dogs."

"What they huntin' for?"

"Coon most likely."

"No, they ain't. They're huntin' for us."

"Dogs won't tetch humans."

"Might be wolves."

"Ain't ary a wolf in Pike County."

"Might be specter hounds."

"Ain't no sech a thing as a specter hound."

Again the dogs took up the cry, but this time farther and fainter.

Tildy and Jeremiah had lost track of the bees while listening to the dogs. Now, tired and dejected, they found a mossy log on which to rest. They were far from home, deep in a tangle of trees all writhen and gnarled. They had miles of hazel thicks and rip-shank cat briars to retrace, a river to wade, and hills and valleys to traverse before they might once again hear friendly voices and see welcome lamplight. And now, at the very last, they had lost their bees. It had occurred to Jeremiah that grown men sometimes hunted weeks for a bee tree.

"Please, Jerry."

"No, I ain't agoin' to quit."

"We might die—them were human bones, I bet."

"Forty years in the wilderness. That's how long it took Moses."

"That's a terrible long time."

"Found the land of milk and honey, didn't he? . . . Kept agoin' till he found his bee tree?"

"God led him," Tildy said.

"God's aleadin' us," Jerry said; "them bees are a pillar of cloud by day and fire by night."

"There ain't no bees and there ain't no pillar," Tildy said, "and we're lost."

Above them in the branch of a high tree they saw a bee martin that some folks call a kingbird. Granny had told Jeremiah it was the bravest bird in the world, a regular cock-of-the-walk, ready to fight a crow or even an eagle. It was surely a double sign to discover at this moment a bird so brave and one that sometimes lived on bees.

"See that leetle gray bird?"

"I seen lots of 'em—they're bee martins."

"And it's catching a bee."

"Uh huh . . . Let's go home, Jerry."

"You ain't listenin' good, Tildy. I said 'a bee.' And there's another and another . . . And, Tildy . . ."

"Uh huh."

"There's the bee tree." Jeremiah leaped to his feet, pointing with wild excitement to an enormous old cottonwood. "See where the bees go in?"

Sure enough, high on the dying trunk was a hole no bigger than a silver dollar into which a ribbon of laden bees was disappearing.

"We've found it, Tildy. We've found it."

"You're wonderful," Tildy said. She felt like laughing and crying at the same time.

Jerry ran to the tree. With trembling fingers he opened his knife.

"You cain't cut down that old whopper with your jackknife."

"Jest carving my initials."

"What for?"

"So every bee-tree hunter in the county'll know this here tree is mine."

Beneath the "J. K." Jeremiah carved "T." for Tildy and "W." for Wheaton.

"Thank you kindly," Tildy said. " 'Tain't my tree by rights. I was jest about ready to start for home."

"Course it's yours jest as much as mine," Jerry said, "and Danny's too." He cut a big "D." below the other letters. Then, as an afterthought, he carved a big heart around them all.

They lost their way in the dusk-dark going home. Luckily the light held until they were out of the swamp and across the little river, but after that they could only guess at the hills and valleys, guiding themselves as best they could by the sunset's afterglow, and later still by the stars. The belt and sword shone forth flashing great jewels. The dewy dipper was cupped with darkness, its outer rim pointing to the faint north star. Even so they had mistaken their way. They came down Bean Blossom Creek to the millpond, skirted it fearfully, but saw no sign of life around the mill.

At last they saw lantern light ahead and heard Granny's old voice crying shrilly, "Jeremiah! Tildy!"

"Tildy! Jeremiah!" called Uncle Hiram.

"Coming!" the children shouted; "here we are."

Happy and muddy, tired and torn, they walked into the pool of lantern light; into the warm circle of fear-sharpened affection. Samantha had been nearly crazy with worry, and Uncle Hiram, sent by Tildy's mother to find the children, was more stern than they had ever seen him.

"Sech bad young'uns," cried Granny, shaking Jeremiah gently by the shoulders.

"But, Granny, we found the biggest bee tree in Indiana."

"You had us plumb frazzled worryin'.'"

"Ain't you goin' to forgive us?" Tildy asked, looking up at Granny with big, pleading eyes shining from her mud-smeared face.

"Wal," said Granny, "seein' you found a bee tree."

"And the biggest in Indiana," said Uncle Hiram, relenting.

"Supper's been awaitin' three hours," Samantha said; "better wash up and get to the table. Me, I'm too wore out to eat a bite."

Between great chunks of johnnycake and long drinks of cold milk they told of their exciting day.

"We had to find it, Granny, so's we could take Danny to the fair," Tildy explained.

"Iffen the biggest bee tree in Indiana ain't a fairgoin' sign from the Almighty . . ." Jeremiah began.

"Could be," Granny admitted, "supposin' thar's honey in it."

"Course there's honey in it," Uncle Hiram said. "Don't be so carn-sarned ornery, Samantha."

"I reckon it maught be a sign," Granny sighed, then added, "Yo're a pair of rascals, but I'd ruther have you pert and chipper than puny and ailin'. . . . I guess yo're the leastest young'uns ever found a bee tree. Better git this child back to her maw, Hiram, afore the poor woman throws a fit."

Long before sunup, before the first cock had frightened the stars, while rosy worms still lay in the dewy grass, Jerry heard the rattle of a jolt wagon that could be none other than Uncle Hiram's. He leaped from his bed, dashed cold water from the garlanded pitcher on the washstand into the rose-adorned washbowl, dabbed as little as he dared of the cold wetness upon his face and hands, and dried himself on the towel. In less than two minutes he was into his shirt and homespun breeches and down the ladder.

Samantha, who had been restless much of the night, was up before him and had bacon and pancakes on the griddle. Jerry noticed that the table was set for three.

"Have a bite of victuals, Hiram," Granny called from the door, wiping her hands on her apron. "Need somethin' to stick to yore ribs while yo're asawin' down that bee tree."

"Thank you kindly," said Uncle Hiram, tying his horse to the hitching post. "Sure I won't be robbing?"

"Plenty for all," said Granny.

Most mornings Jerry would have eaten his button-popping fill of buckweat cakes and homemade maple syrup with crisp rashers of home-cured bacon. This morning he could scarcely wait to scrape his plate and hit the road. But Samantha was filled with warnings and premonitions and insisted on speaking her mind.

"Reckon you remember what killed Josiah Tarleton?" Granny said as she heaped the pancakes on Hiram's willow ware plate. "Smashed him flat as one of them griddlecakes; busted pretty near every bone in his body."

"I'd ruther not talk about it," Uncle Hiram protested gently, " 'specially at mealtimes."

"Wal, yo're cutting down a tree, ain't you?" said Granny, serving the sizzling bacon, "and a fallin' tree mashed and mangled old Josiah . . . Lord in Heaven, were he a gory mess. I allus said liftin' that oak tree offen his mortal enemy were what killed my poor David."

"We'll be extra careful, Samantha," Hiram promised. "I'm a better axman than Josiah were, if I do say it."

"I'll be aworryin' every minute yo're gone," Granny sighed. "Seems like somethin' turrible allus happens to those near and dear to me. Thirteen years ago last January it were when David heard him cryin' for help other side of the fence—never should of tried to lift that tree with his hurt back and all . . ."

"Now, Samantha," Uncle Hiram admonished, "you'll be givin' yourself and the boy nightmares."

"I never heered tell about Grandpap Kincaid arescuin' Grandpap Tarleton," Jeremiah said.

"I were savin' it for a story kiver," Granny said.

"Right way to break it gentle were in a song ballad, but seein' yo're sawin' down a big tree . . ."

"We'll be careful, Granny."

"Did my Christian duty, if I do say it," Samantha added defensively; "helped David tote that big, wicked feller right to his own bed. Helped wash the mortal gorm off his poor, busted body, with Lafe ahidin' out in the woods somewhere like a scared hunted thing, and his own daughter Arabella off Lord knows where, not even livin' with her own husband, Seth. . . . That were a terrible year."

"Stop tormentin' yourself," Uncle Hiram pleaded.

"Where were my mam?" Jeremiah asked in a small voice.

"Oh, she were livin' high, wide, and handsome," Granny said; "never did come back to help bury her pap. . . . Nobody to close his eyes except Samantha Kincaid; and he tellin' me he had allus loved me with his dyin' breath. . . . Have some more griddlecakes, Hiram?"

"Thank you just the same."

"Oh, that were a terrible year," Granny said. "My David hurt his poor crippled back aliftin' on that tree, took a misery in his chest from gettin' wet and cold while helping his neighbor like a good Samaritan. Tuk to his bed and died in three months—jest when the dogwood was in bloom. He allus loved the dogwood and the redbud . . . More cakes for you, Jeremiah?"

"I don't feel so good, Granny."

"Gotta eat if yo're agoin' to grow," Granny said. "Now take good care of yoreselves while yo're cuttin' down that bee tree. I don't want no more funeralizin' in this family."

"Yore granny," Uncle Hiram observed as they started off in the jolt wagon, "never does things by halves. It's whole hog or none. She's the worryin', sermonizin' sort of woman. She'd give you the last stitch offen her own body, the last bite of victuals in her cupboard. She's a good Christian woman who's allus done her duty as she seen it and accordin' to her lights, but now and then I wish she'd shut that

116

old mouth of hers, or jest use it for eatin' griddle-cakes."

Through the long, dark tunnel of his brooding thoughts Jeremiah glimpsed the light no larger than a candle which was suddenly large as the rim of the sun now peeking over the horizon. That joyous light—fair as the Easter Resurrection after the darkness of the tomb—was the memory of his bee tree and the reason for the present pilgrimage. Much as the earth shakes off the dreariness of winter when spring flowers arise, his spirit left behind the dark memories Samantha had just confided and soared ahead to visions of wild honey.

"Where we picking up Tildy?"

"Her maw said she couldn't come. Put her foot down like she meant it."

Clouds soft as goose down caught the rising sun. Trees were silhouetted in jet bars across the huge ruddy disk of the sun. The valleys were still secret with low-hung mist as this one-horse cavalcade clop-clopped through the fresh morning air by a back road to Dead Man's Swamp. Uncle Hiram knew an ancient stretch of corduroy once used for an old logging road that might bring them near the tree. They crossed the dark little river at a shallow ford and turned down this long-unused trail into the swamp.

"It's right in here somewhere," Jerry said. "Here's where we waded across."

And there, sure enough, rising above the foliage at some little distance was the enormous half-dead cotton-wood.

"Sure that's it, son?"

"There's my initials," Jerry said as they drew nearer.

"Got our day cut out for us, Jeremiah."

As they unloaded the ax and saws from the jolt wagon, a sad thought came to Jeremiah.

"You reckon trees can see and feel and hear same as humans?"

117

"I ain't absolutely, positively certain," Uncle Hiram said, "but chances are they cain't."

The thought lingered, however, in the back of his mind as Hiram's razor-sharp ax began to take the first big bites out of the bole, sending up chips like frightened quail flushed from cover.

Jeremiah thought that maybe the old cottonwood no longer wished to live, being gray with age and weary with holding up its vast limbs. He could see that woodpeckers and sapsuckers had drilled the bark in search of insects. Squirrels had probably nested in the hollow branches. Certainly bees had patiently built their curious six-sided cells in orderly rows to store the sunshine of summer.

The tree, Jerry thought, must be tired of the chatter of jays and the death watch of turkey buzzards (who always chose such a lookout). Maybe it wanted to die.

"First you make a big notch on the side you want to drop it," Uncle Hiram explained. "Quite a few tricks to this trade."

It was a marvel to see Uncle Hiram place his strokes, first from above, then from below, with each swing of the ax taking off a chip the size of your hand and half an inch thick. He had planned to fell the tree where it would do the least damage to the saplings around it. And he bragged to Jeremiah he could place it within five feet of the spot he had chosen.

When the notch was deep enough, Jerry and Hiram began making a saw cut on the other side of the bole. They moved back and forth in a slow rhythm like church music. The green light filtered down through the tall trees; a bend in the river flashed in the morning sun; and the old cottonwood whispered in the wind, remembering two hundred years of winter storm and summer leaf.

While they sawed, Jeremiah asked many questions, the answers to which were as needful to his growth as food or drink. Between puffs on his pipe, Uncle Hiram answered as best he was able.

Where does the wind come from? Why are some flowers blue and some red or yellow? Why do birds

118

fly south in the fall and north in the spring? It wasn't always easy to answer Jeremiah's questions because they were never the idle, babbling sort. They had to do with all creation: with time and space and the moon and the stars; with the world's beginning and with his own. At last he came to the question he had wanted to ask all along:

"What did Granny mean about my mam?"

"Wal," Uncle Hiram said, "it's quite a story. And I'm agoin' to tell it afore yore granny mixes you up worse than you're mixed already. First off, get this straight: there ain't one thing about your mam to be ashamed of."

And so Jeremiah learned about his mother during the long hours they spent sawing down the great tree. She had been born during the first years of Josiah's marriage to Lilith; a bright, active, willful little redhead, as full of curiosity as a chipmunk. From the first she had loved to go with her mother on walks through the woods. Very early she had been given lessons on the violin. She didn't need lessons to learn to ride any horse on the place at breakneck speed, often bareback and always astride. Josiah Tarleton had pampered her during her childhood, in the days before he had lost most of his money and part of his mind.

"Lafe was a worry," Uncle Hiram said. "Cain't tell when a moonling'll turn out dangerous. Lilith taught both young'uns to read and write—but the one was moody and slow; the other bright and skittery. After Lilith died, Josiah jest gave up and let 'em run."

"Wisht I could play the fiddle and ride a fast horse like my mam," Jerry said.

"Your pap was jest as admirin'," Uncle Hiram said approvingly, refilling his pipe. "Fact, Arabella had him eatin' out of her hand."

Hiram grew thoughtful and silent as they returned to their sawing, but the next time they rested, he went to the heart of the matter.

"Guess those two young folks was plumb fed up with Cat Hollow and Fulton Corners," he said; "cain't say I could blame 'em—families feudin' back and forth. Nothin' much to do for a livin'. They wanted out— so off they went without much more than a fiddle and a race horse between 'em—both belongin' to Arabella."

It was a strange story Uncle Hiram told the boy. Jeremiah's father had a fine voice, his mother played the violin. They entertained at county fairs, they worked on showboats, sometimes they left their beloved mare named "Spinny" with Arabella's Grandfather Henderson—a very old man by that time who lived near Louisville and still kept fine horses. He had never forgiven Lilith for marrying Josiah, but he made it up by taking the even more willful Arabella to his heart.

"Sure they gambled, bet on races, lived a life your granny figgered was plumb sinful. They burned their candle at both ends, as the saying goes, and they left you for your granny to raise. They died like they lived—brave and careless."

"What were my mam doin' she oughtn't that year both grandpaps died?"

"Wal," Uncle Hiram said, "she were jest spirited and spunky. . . . I'd better let your granny tell you that story; reckon I've talked too much already. . . ."

"I ain't got ary a thing to remember my mam by," Jerry mourned.

"Son, you've got the whole of creation to remember her by. Birds, and blossom boughs in the spring, and runnin' water, and fiddle music. Somebody's still got your mam's fiddle most likely."

"Wish I had my mam's fiddle," Jeremiah said, "I'd learn me them pieces she plays when she comes back nights. . . . She's tryin' to give me fiddle lessons. I know it in my bones."

Using the blade of a second and smaller saw he had brought along, Hiram played a bit of Granny's new ballad, striking the notes with the bowl of his pipe:

> *O, a ribbon-bow to bind her hair,*
> *A kerchief for her weeping,*
> *A golden ring for her finger fair*
> *To shine as she lay sleeping. . . .*

Saw music there in the green wilderness seemed like far bells and birdsong and water running over shallows. It went well with the memory of fiddle music played by a ghost.

"Time we finished our job of sawin', Jerry," Uncle Hiram said as the last note died away.

He began to talk about bees—workers, queens, and drones—about a big swarm he caught once by beating on a tin pan; and how one of Saunders's best horses was plumb stung to death. "Cain't be too careful when bees are swarmin'."

At last the great tree began to sigh.

"Look out, Jerry, she's goin' down."

The ancient cottonwood hesitated a moment, then with a great cry and the tearing of fibers went roaring to earth, hitting the quaking marsh with a sound like thunder. The bees poured from their hole with the anger of any living thing whose home is invaded. But Hiram was ready to light the oil-soaked rags on the end of a long pole and "whop 'em with smoke." The heavy fumes soon quieted the bees until they reeled in sullen stupor into the marsh grass. A few moments' work with the ax now lay open the hollow trunk where gleamed hundreds of pounds of dark comb honey garnered from countless millions of wild blossoms. It was the richest bee tree Uncle Hiram had ever seen, enough to fill the four washtubs he had optimistically placed in the box of the jolt wagon.

"Oh, Uncle Hiram. Ain't it a splendid sight?"

"If this ain't the fair-goin' sign," Uncle Hiram said, "then the Almighty's fresh out of signs and portents."

"We'll fotch it right down to Pete Grundy's."

"Purtiest lot of sweetenin' I ever tasted," Hiram said, offering Jeremiah a clean chip for a spoon; "clover and locust mostly."

"You reckon I'm rich, Uncle Hiram?"

121

"Well, maybe John D.'s a mite richer. But least-ways you got the wherewithal to ride on the cars to the County Fair. Right nice-tastin', ain't it?"

As they jogged along, tired and happy, Hiram made up some verses for the occasion:

> *"Jerry Kincaid he sat on a bee,*
> *Follered him home to a cottonwood tree;*
> *Folks gonna call him 'honey hound,'*
> *Richest bee tree ever found."*

"Sing another verse, Uncle Hiram."
"Hold yore horses, son. I'm athinkin' one up.

> *"Clear the road, 'cause we ain't braggin'*
> *So much honey the wagon's saggin'.*
> *Jerry Kincaid's a millionaire,*
> *Money to burn at the County Fair."*

They had chosen a short cut to Fulton Corners which was now taking them directly past Tildy's house.

"Remember, half of it's Tildy's," Jerry said.

"Tildy," Hiram shouted, pulling his horse to a stop. "We got somethin' to show you."

Mrs. Wheaton came out, her tired eyes squinting at the sunlight, her ever-busy fingers continuing to baste a hem while she talked. She scolded Jerry gently for taking Tildy so far on such a wild-goose chase.

"Where's Tildy now, Mrs. Wheaton?"

"She teased and she begged," the harassed woman explained, "so I let her go out to your place, Jeremiah."

"Tildy's goin' to be rich," Jerry said; "look at all this honey."

And despite herself the seamstress was impressed at the brimming tubs of light brown comb dripping with amber sweetness. She wished them luck with the sale of their loot.

As they drove up to the hitching rail at Grundy's store, Uncle Hiram was singing:

> *"Tap your cash drawer, old Pete Grundy,*
> *Here we come on lucky Monday . . ."*

" 'Tain't Monday, it's Tuesday," Grundy said.

"Gotta make it rhyme, don't I?" Hiram asked:

> *"Dime a pound for tubs of gold*
> *Aged in a bee tree twelve years old."*

As though it were traintime, curious citizens poured from every house to see Jerry's treasure. They put exploratory fingers into the tubs and licked them critically while shaking their heads with amazement.

"Land sakes," a farm wife exclaimed, "all out of one tree?"

"Bees been amakin' that since you was born, Jerry," her husband said.

"Help me with these tubs, Fud."

"Aw, Paw, they're heavy."

"Yes, and yer fat and lazy," Pete Grundy said; "get a move on."

One by one the tubs were weighed on the platform scale, with Uncle Hiram keeping his own score.

"Let's see, at ten cents a pound," the storekeeper figured, " 'fraid it comes to twenty-two dollars. You're goin' to bust me, Jeremiah."

"Didn't cheat you a penny," Uncle Hiram approved.

"Never cheat nobody," said Pete Grundy dourly, peeling twenty-two singles from a roll in his pocket.

"My land, look at that cash money," the farm woman sighed.

"Always knowed he was a smart young'un," crowed Grandpa Meeker.

"Wastin' his time, was I?" Pete Grundy asked.

"Gee," Arch McCoy said. "Now you're rich, Jerry."

"Guess I'd better give up my job and hunt bee trees," Bob Peters observed. "What you going to do with all that cash, Jerry?"

"I'm takin' my prize lamb to the County Fair."

"What prize, booby prize?" Fud Grundy asked.

Jerry slowly put his money in his pocket and clenched his fists. He felt that he had grown stronger during the summer, and quite suddenly he was no longer afraid of Fud.

"Think you're smart, don'tcha?" Fud said. He pushed Jerry so violently that he fell backward, hitting his head against the store. Into Jeremiah's mind came the story of David and Goliath. He remembered how the shepherd boy had defeated the giant because he had faith. Leaping to his feet, he lowered his head and charged into Fud, catching him squarely in the pit of the stomach. Fud stumbled backward and sat neatly in the center of a tub of honey. He howled with surprise and anger while the crowd roared with laughter. Fud tried to wipe the tears from his face but only managed to smear himself with honey and comb.

The screen door flew open, bell tinkling, and out raced Grundy, red-faced with rage. He dragged his son out of the tub by the scruff of the neck, shouting:

"Hold still, you darn fool. That stuff cost ten cents a pound."

Balancing the dripping boy over the tub, he scraped what he could back into the container. "Don't worry, folks. I'll send this tub to the city."

Jerry reached in his pocket to be certain that his money was safe. Then he walked proudly to the jolt wagon. To himself he was singing:

> "Faith—faith—
> You gotter have faith;
> The Good Book saith
> You gotter have faith."

9 PRIDE GOETH BEFORE . . .

Jeremiah could not say he had not been warned. From Proverbs and from Ecclesiastes he knew the danger of pride and the folly of hope. Yet as he rode toward Cat Hollow with Uncle Hiram, the world seemed no bigger than a marble and safe in his pocket. Solomon in all his glory was never so rich nor so happy as Jeremiah Kincaid.

"What's bigger'n a county fair, Uncle Hiram?"

"State fair."

"What's bigger'n a state fair?"

"Wal, once in a while there's a world's fair."

"With blue ribbons for prize lambs?"

"I reckon."

"Now iffen I use my cash money to traipse to the County Fair, 'n' then my County Fair prize money to go to the State Fair, 'n' then my State Fair prize money to go to the World's Fair, and . . ."

"Hold on there, son! 'Pears to me you're gettin' a little ahead of yourself. You ain't even got to the County Fair yet."

125

"Granny jest cain't say 'No,' can she, Uncle Hiram, now I found a bee tree and got all this money?"

"Granny can always say 'No'—she's the no-sayin'est woman in Pike County."

"Then I'll go all alone by my ownself," Jeremiah threatened darkly. "It's my money and my lamb."

"Goin' all alone, are you?"

"Take you with me, of course."

"Much obliged. How about Tildy?"

"And Tildy, of course. Hear what Pete Grundy said? Biggest bee tree he ever heard tell of."

"I told you that 'fore Grundy did."

"Guess I showed old Fud Grundy. Guess he won't never double-dare me agin."

"Don't get too big for your britches, son," Uncle Hiram said, tousling Jeremiah's hair. "As Granny'd say, 'Pride goeth before destruction.'"

And just at that moment they heard Granny's worried voice from afar calling:

"Tildy . . . Til-dy-y."

Hiram pulled sharply on the reins.

"Whoa, boy."

He stood up in the jolt wagon and shouted:

"Hal-looo! Hal-looo! That you, Granny Kincaid?"

"That's Granny, right enough," Jerry said.

"Sounds real worried," Uncle Hiram said. "Over this way, Samantha," he shouted between his cupped hands.

A few moments later Granny's troubled face appeared above the brambled hedgerow.

"You ain't seen Tildy?"

"Aw, Tildy kin take keer of herself," Jerry said. "She's around somewhars. Look, Granny! Look at all this cash money."

Granny came through a break in the hedge and approached the jolt wagon.

"What's wrong, Samantha?"

"I've been trampin' the woods more'n two hours, shoutin' myself hoarse."

"Know how much money I got here?" Jerry asked, holding his roll of bills toward Granny.

126

"Land sakes, not now," Granny said with annoyance, pushing his hand away.

"But, Granny, look. We kin go to the fair. The Lord *gave* me a sign."

"Lord gave me a different kind of sign," Granny said. "Lamb's lost and so's the girl."

"Tildy's lost?" Uncle Hiram puzzled. "What happened?"

"Cain't rightly say. She was gettin' Danny a rack of clover. Next thing I know, lamb's gone and girl's gone—clover strewed to kingdom come. Gate wide open."

"She let Danny git away?" Jeremiah wailed.

"That's what I figger," Granny said; "ain't nobody around here mean enough to do it apurpose—or is there?" She peered up-hollow toward the Tarleton farm.

"Course not," Uncle Hiram said; "purely an accident. Girl left the gate ajar and the critter bolted for the tall timber."

"With Tildy after him," Granny said. "Makes the most sense . . . Poor young'un. She's still arunnin' through the woods atryin' to ketch it, most likely."

"Gee whiz," Jerry said, "why'd you let her do it, Granny? Which way'd they go? Gee whiz, I gotta find my lamb."

"Devil take yore lamb," said Granny. "We gotta find the girl—found her hair ribbon by the snake fence, up-creek. Tuft of black wool on a splintered rail."

"Danny, Dannnn-nn-ny," Jeremiah cried, jumping out of the wagon and starting up-creek.

"You hunt for Tildy," Granny shouted after him. "Never mind the lamb."

"Tildy kin find her way anywhars," Jerry shouted back. "I gotta find my lamb." His voice ended on a frightened sob as he disappeared among the trees.

"Don't worry about Tildy, I'll find her," Uncle Hiram comforted; "but first I'm takin' you home, Samantha. You're pretty near tuckered out." He helped her into the jolt wagon and clucked to the horse. For a few minutes they jogged along without talk, each deep in his own thoughts. It wasn't all strawberries and cream raising a girl, a boy, and a lamb. One thing one day and another the next. The breathless summer afternoon was almost too quiet to suit Hiram's fancy. He didn't like the yellow haze gathering in the west.

"They *would* go up Bean Blossom Creek," said Granny, breaking the silence.

"Aworryin' about Lafe Tarleton agin?"

"Allus was troublesome folk."

"Lafe wouldn't lay a hand to them young'uns," Hiram said.

"Cain't never trust a Tarleton."

As they turned in at Samantha's cabin one of their worries was lightened, for there came Tildy stumbling up the lane from the pasture. Her dress was torn and wet and her face was streaked with dirt and tears. But at least she was back in one piece, although sobbing as though her heart would break.

Uncle Hiram handed the reins to Samantha, jumped down from the wagon, and ran to scoop the little girl up in his arms.

"Now, now, Tildy," he said soothingly.

"Lord Almighty, baby, you had me *that* worried," Granny chided.

"It's my fault, it's all my fault," Tildy wailed.

"Could of happened to anybody," Hiram said.

"I shoulda fastened the gate behind me . . . and then Old 99 blew its whistle and scared Danny . . . I called and called . . . I went 'way up the creek . . . and then I heard them dogs ahowlin'."

"My, yo're soaked to the skin," Granny said. "Lucky it's a warm day."

"I fell down in the crick too," Tildy sobbed.

"Git her home and into some dry clothes," Granny said to Hiram. "Tell her maw to rub goose grease on her chest jest in case."

"Yes'm," said Hiram, putting Tildy on the wagon seat. "But what about Jeremiah? That looks like a storm blowing up."

"You git Tildy to her maw 'fore she comes down

with a chill. Here, wrap this old shawl around her. Jeremiah kin fend for himself."

The killdeers were crying "killdeer, killdeer"—a sure warning of rain—as Jeremiah started on his quest. Soon they changed their cry to "poor dear, poor dear"—meaning, of course, the lamb now strayed from the fold.

The air was breathless and oppressive; not even the narrow pennants of green along the willow boughs stirred in the dangerous silence. Then the wind freshened, lifting last year's lightly drifted flotsam into hissing whirls from dry sand bars in the creek, silvering the willows and poplars, making the aspens quake with fear. The wind caught in old Andrew Jackson's sparse mane, blowing his forelock jauntily over one eye and urging him to kick up his heels like a two-year-old. The wind burrowed through the pasture grass like a woodchuck running for its hole; ruffled the untroubled pool at the bend of the creek.

It urged Jeremiah in his race against fear; gave him the energy to leap the stream where he had never been able to leap it before; carried him forward like a runaway kite toward the Tarleton fence. Yes, surely the lamb had come this way, for here on a tangle of briars and there on a splintered rail were smidgins of black wool. And here in the leafmold was a cloven hoofprint.

Faint as a wheel upon a distant bridge, then deep as boulders tumbling from the hills, the thunder murmured, gathered voice, and spoke.

It might have been the deep rumble of Jehovah's own words spoken in warning to Jeremiah. The storm, like the fact of the lamb's escape, was certainly God's displeasure—His angry sign. Yes, surely Granny was right. He had taken Jeremiah's only lamb as He had once threatened to take Abraham's beloved son, Isaac, for reasons Jerry could not easily imagine. Finding the bee tree and earning the cash money had been a false portent, a mistaken prophecy of the future. More real than the twenty-two dollars still in his pocket was the undeniable truth that Danny was lost and a storm was rising. The Almighty was wroth.

But His ways were inscrutable and difficult to unravel. Why, if God were willing to heed even the sparrow's fall, if He were more concerned over one lost lamb than over all those safe in the fold, was He now angered because of similar concern in the heart of a boy? Thus Jeremiah, plunging through a darkening world, argued with himself in a maze of doubt.

Heat lightning trembled along the horizon; birds went to cover with sharp notes of fear. The light was sulphur-yellow among the boles of the beeches and sycamores. The thunder growled like something ready to pounce. But against this anger Jeremiah's mind followed the black letter of Granny's old Bible, as from memory he searched the Gospel according to St. Matthew:

"How think ye? If a man have an hundred sheep, and one of them be gone astray, doth he not leave the ninety and nine, and goeth into the mountains, and seeketh that which is gone astray?"

The thunder crashed again, this time very near at hand. A bolt of blinding intensity ripped a thirty-foot strip of bark from a hickory tree, leaving a smoking scar of livid white along the wounded trunk. A limb crashed too near for comfort. Over the valley rolled the wheels of the chariots of the enemy.

"Danny, Danny—come, Danny, Danny," the boy cried. But as though to counter him at every turn the thunder spoke again, drowning his anxious voice. There could be no doubt of the Lord's displeasure.

Jeremiah did not see the dark figure standing near the mill watching his progress up the creek bottom. He was too deep in his argument with the Almighty, too anxious to find and shelter his endangered lamb. The words of St. Matthew continued in his mind:

"And if so be that he find it, verily I say unto you, he rejoiceth more of that sheep than of the ninety and nine which went not astray."

130

As Granny had once told him in a moment of wisdom, it is easy to quote the New Testament against the Old Testament Jehovah. But no more dangerous procedure could be imagined. For it was the Old Testament Jehovah, beloved of Granny, who had said, "Vengeance is mine." Such thoughts were terrifying here in the Tarleton woods loud with thunder and the rush of rain. This was no moment to say, "With thine own words, Lord, I defy Thee."

Yet in a voice whipped away on the compelling wind he cried: "Danny, Danny—where are you, boy?"

Was he being tested like Job? If he endured, would he be rewarded? A mighty rush of wind caught Jeremiah in its strong arms. Struggling through the tumult and up the rapidly rising creek, he continued to cry:

"Danny, Danny—where are you, boy?"

Wave upon wave of wind and water seemed to be overwhelming him, as in the beginning when the earth was without form and void, and darkness was upon the face of the deep. But through this storm Jeremiah continued firm in his decision to find his lamb, crying, "Danny, Danny—come, Danny, Danny, Danny," his small voice thin and determined against the surge of rain and thunder.

It was a fortunate thing that the man standing in the lee of the mill watching this uneven contest saw the boy pushed by a cyclonic burst of wind headlong into the raging brook, saw him strike his head against the boulder, and swirl into the current.

10 THE ODYSSEY OF THE LOST LAMB

Tildy had walked out to Cat Hollow that morning to await the return of Jeremiah and Uncle Hiram from Dead Man's Swamp. How much honey would they bring? And would Granny Kincaid now relent and let them go to the fair? Wisely, Tildy refrained from bringing up a subject so controversial as the fair, but instead praised Granny for her "Cat Hollow Wedding" cover on which she was putting the finishing touches.

"I've wove me a sermon into this-here kiver," Granny said.

"What kind of a sermon, Granny?"

"A hell's-fire-and-brimstone, revival-meetin' sizzler agin horse racin', gamblin', and traipsin' fiddlin' women."

"Who you apreachin' at, Granny?"

"I'm apreachin' at Jeremiah; maybe I'm apreachin' at you, Tildy."

"I ain't done ary a wicked thing, Granny. Neither has Jeremiah."

"Stitch in time saves nine," said Granny. "Cain't

start too soon sendin' young'uns up the straight and narrer . . ."

"That's real purty weavin'," Tildy said. "Who's the bride?"

"Arabella Tarleton."

"Who's the groom?"

"Seth Kincaid."

"What for's the preacher got those funny little horns in his hair?"

"That's the devil atyin' the weddin' knot."

"Ain't Seth and Arabella the pap and mam of Jeremiah?"

"Course they was."

"What you tryin' to do, scare the livin' daylights out of Jerry?"

"Tildy, I'm aimin' to preach God into that boy so that no traipsin' women can conjure him off like his mam conjured his pap."

"Sounds like a real excitin' story."

"I've dreamed me some new verses for my ballad song," Granny said. "I'll sing 'em to Jerry first chanct I git."

"Sing 'em to me, Granny."

"Wal, seein' I'm sermonizin' both of you . . ." Granny's voice was still sweet and clear:

> *"The witchy lass moved o'er the grass*
> *Nor touched her silver shoon—*
> *The stars were purties in her hair,*
> *Her ribbond the new moon.*
>
> *"Oh follow me, oh follow me!*
> *Her eyes were fox-fire gleaming;*
> *Her fiddle-tune came down the wind*
> *And set the young lad dreaming.*
>
> *"I'll follow you in the evening dew,*
> *I'll follow through the night;*
> *I'll follow where the fox-fire gleams*
> *In yore two eyes so bright."*

Now Granny changed her bright, sunlit morning song to a slow dirge, like funeral music, and sang:

> *"On a lonely knoll is a bury hole*
> *Where the twain will rest for aye.*
> *And the silver shoon will traipse no more*
> *To lure lads off to die."*

"That's a real sad ballad song," said Tildy, wiping her eyes with a corner of her apron. "What happened to Jeremiah's mam and pap? Why did they die?"

But Granny had set her mouth firmly. She had her own way of telling a tale or preaching a sermon and she was not to be hurried.

"In the Lord's good time," said Granny dreamily. All the bitterness had gone out of her voice and a tender smile flickered at the corners of her mouth as she finger-wove two intertwining roses locked above the white headstones of Seth and Arabella on the counterpane.

After a while Tildy grew restless. She went out to gather clover to feed Danny while she waited for the return of Uncle Hiram and Jeremiah. The lamb was acting like a six-weeks colt in pasture. Poor Danny. Ever since he had been put in his new sturdy pen he had been testing every inch of the fence trying to open a path to freedom. But the fence was very high, and the posts did not budge when he pushed against them with his round woolly head. The heavy boards were tightly nailed to those solid locust posts. Remembering his wild romps with Jeremiah, he was merely biding his time, awaiting his first chance to make a dash for the carefree, sunlit world beyond the fence.

Tildy should have noticed Danny's mood. She should have been more careful when she went in through the gate with her basket of clover. But she was still dreaming of Granny's ballad song and not putting more than half her mind on her work.

The young ram saw the gate open a crack, made one bound for it, and was out in the wide world aching for adventure. He bucked and cavorted, bleated joyously, went up in the air and came down

134

stiff-legged. Even so, Tildy might have caught him had it not been for the shrill blast of the train as Old 99 came up the track.

Danny thought of himself as the bravest thing in fleece. But the fierce challenge of that whistle addled his brain and scared what wits he had completely out of him. The long-drawn, piercing wail of the locomotive impaled him like a locust thorn, making his fine wool stiffen with fear, and ice water trickle down his spine from the base of his horns to the stub of his tail.

Instinctively he leaped a boulder, careened around the corner of the barn, and started down the lane as though pursued by a nest of hornets. He reached the pasture at a dead gallop and headed up Bean Blossom Creek as though little black demons were nestled in his wool jabbing him with tiny pitchforks.

Behind him came Tildy, pleading and crying. But her frightened voice only made him run the harder, kicking the sod out from under him in long green waves of retreating turf. Danny was no longer a mere "smidgin of lampblack." He was a powerful young ram, spirited and able. As he settled into his stride, the little stones flew back from his polished hoofs, the air flowed into his lungs in delicious long draughts, and he felt the muscles of his sturdy legs working like smooth machinery under his fleecy hide.

What if he did leave wisps of black wool on the tumble-down rail fence? He was out of the pasture now and into a wilderness of deep green silence, far from the whistle of the train, safe from all pursuers. He heard his name being called ever fainter and farther behind him. But it was not the one voice that might have brought him meekly back to pasture and to pen.

Danny didn't think very much or very clearly. But he knew hot from cold; light from dark; fear from pleasure. He didn't know whether he ran because he was afraid, or was afraid because he ran. But certainly he ate because he was hungry; he wasn't hungry because he ate. At the very least he was smarter and

135

stronger than any of the white lambs in the Kincaid pasture. Anyone who thought he was woolly-witted merely because he was woolly-headed would have made a grave error.

The whistle of a train, the bark of a dog, or the crash of thunder and lightning made him want to flee. He could find water as any animal can, and it was unlikely that he would eat deadly nightshade or other poison berries. He knew his head was made to butt with and his little horns to hook with. So if any young ram had a chance alone in the hills it was Danny Kincaid, the brightest lamb in Cat Hollow.

Danny stopped beside a fern-fringed spring of lonesome water which reflected his own bright-eyed, blunt-nosed face (framed among fleecy clouds in the blue sky high above him). He drew the cold, mint-fresh water deeply into his throat, enjoying every thirst-quenching swallow. He raised his dewy nostrils from the spring to listen intently, then drank again. What was that whorl of purple bloom over his right ear? When he looked more closely at his reflection in the water he saw that he was wearing a thistle blossom held fast in the tightly curled wool beside his oiled and gleaming little horn. If lambs could laugh, Danny would have chuckled. A gay and carefree lamb was he, adorned with flowers and starting on the biggest adventure of his young life.

It was beautiful for the first hour or two. The golden summer sunlight filtered down through the great beeches, dappling the leafmold which was deliciously yielding underfoot yet dry enough to break cleanly from his polished hoofs. The woods were filled with dozens of new odors, very few of them alarming. He sampled various leaves and flowers, approving particularly of vetch with its purple pealike blossoms.

Being a spring lamb, he thought there would always be fresh clover to eat. He had never seen autumn leaves fall, nor snow come drifting over the hills. Being an orphan, so to speak, no ewe had told him of the bitter nights when sheep huddle in little flocks for warmth. He had never watched the ice send delicate

136

spear points over each clear pool to seal at last each waterhole. Gathering food for winter seemed a silly pastime to this carefree lamb. He was convinced that as long as he wished to wander in these hills, the weather would be warm and sunny, the pasturage plentiful, and the breezes as gentle as the caress of Jeremiah's hand.

Thinking vaguely of Jeremiah, he was sad for a moment. A cloud had blown across the sun, and a sharp, whirling little breeze came sidling up the hill, ruffling his fleece and playing tag with his small ears. Leaves twisted about him, and far away a dog howled mournfully.

Still Danny was not afraid. If a storm blew up he would find shelter. Far back in his ancestry there were brave Highland sheep, sure of foot and filled with daring, as hardy as their kilted Highland shepherds across the ocean-sea.

Nevertheless, he did not like the sulphur-yellow sky nor the heat lightning which quavered along the horizon like some distant grass fire. And there was a note of warning deep in the throat of the far-off thunder. The squirrels scampered for their hollow tree. The cries of frightened birds awoke similar fear within his own fleecy breast. He watched with dark anticipation the inky clouds like herds of enormous black rams charging up the pastures of the sky.

It wasn't brave. It wasn't what he had planned. But as the first drops of rain began to splatter into the treetops, Danny decided that he had better start for home. He could have sworn that he knew his directions and could back track to the Kincaid pasture. But the swaying trees, the rush of the rain, and the flash and roar of the storm threw him all in a dither. "Woolly-headed *and* woolly-witted," he said to himself with wry humor. It was the last witty remark in which he would indulge for many a day.

Bleating wildly now and thoroughly frightened, he started plunging madly through the hazel brush and sumac, mounting a hill thick with bull briars and dewberry vines. During a momentary lull he heard first one dog, then the pack—nearer now, and hungry for spring lamb.

Sprinting like a mountain goat, he gained the crest of the hill and looked out into the misty, swirling world, cut now and again with jagged blue flashes of lightning that revealed the wide valley below. A wild joy mingled with his fear, as though all that lay below him were his pasture. As though he were already a great ram with a vast flock of ewes waiting for him in the valley—a flock he must watch over and fight for to the death.

But again he heard the dogs, this time very near at hand. Danny turned sharply down a steep ravine which widened into a valley through enormous trees. Soaked with rain and matted with burs, aching with weariness and fighting for breath, the young ram plunged through the storm seeking shelter—a hollow log, a cave to hide in. Once he thought he heard Jeremiah's voice. But again the thunder rolled, drowning all other sound. He did not hear the voice again.

11 BEHOLD, I HAVE DREAMED A DREAM

Although it was still midsummer, Jeremiah dreamed that the chill winds of autumn were sweeping Cat Hollow. Pumpkins were heaped in golden piles between the shocks of corn, and frosty wild grapes burdened the vines.

He could hear his feet shuffling through the dry leaves of autumn (crimson from the maples, buckskin yellow from the hickories). Wedges of southward-flying Canadian geese split the blue October sky, disappearing at last into the haze along the horizon.

But the honking of wild geese, the litter of hickory nuts (like stars of the Milky Way in the sere grass), found no answering joy in his empty heart. He heard his own voice as though it were another's calling, "Danny, Danny." It might have been John the Baptist crying in the wilderness, or his own namesake, Jeremiah, prophesying doom. He saw himself climbing endless hills toward the misty October moon, following the faint promise of distant fiddle music. But the cabins were dark. The music was a will-o'-the-wisp leading him nowhere. Blue-knuckled with chill, he wandered through tall trees sorrowful with wind, calling his lost lamb.

Suddenly the wind grew fainter. Warmth came over him. The fiddle music was nearer now and very clear. He opened his eyes to find a brisk fire burning on a wide hearth. The firelight was glowing upon a violin tucked under a grizzled beard, the bow traveling gracefully, held between the thumb and finger of a great weather-beaten, work-gnarled hand.

Jerry did not remember falling; he knew nothing of the strong arms that had lifted him from the creek and brought him to this room. Instinctively he realized that the fiddler was Lafe Tarleton; that the music sometimes heard far up the hollow came from these fingers and this violin.

Strangely enough he felt no fear; only a sense of wonder and amazement. He remembered, now, that the man before him could not speak. Jeremiah did not wish to shame him, yet before he knew it the question had slipped from the tip of his tongue.

"Yo're Lafe Tarleton, ain't you?"

The big head nodded slowly above the violin.

"You ain't seen my lost lamb?"

The bearded mouth twisted, tried futilely to form a word. Then the head shook slowly from side to side.

As though he were trying to speak to him with fiddle tunes, Lafe Tarleton continued to play the violin, and Jeremiah lay back in his warm blanket watching his clothes steaming on the screen before the fire. As his eyes became accustomed to the half-dark he saw, to his amazement, shelf upon shelf of books set into the dark wood-paneled walls. Jerry figured it would take a person all the days of his life to read those books. But it would be a pure misery not to know what was on every unturned page.

"Kin you read?" Jeremiah asked.

Lafe nodded his head proudly.

"All them books?"

The big man shook his head and looked away. He

put the fiddle on the table and went to the nearest shelf, returning with a sixth-grade *McGuffey's Reader*.

"I ain't that far yet my ownself," Jeremiah said politely. Lafe looked his gratitude, and Jeremiah knew he had made a friend. "Is that my mam's fiddle?"

The grizzled head nodded.

"Kin I touch it?"

Lafe put the violin in the boy's hands.

"It'd pleasure me to fiddle," Jeremiah said wistfully. "Reckon you could teach me?"

Lafe nodded eagerly. He showed Jeremiah how to put the fiddle under his chin and how to hold the bow.

"Take me years and years, most likely," Jeremiah said sadly. "I'll be traipsin' up here every few days for lessons."

A look of wonder and joy spread over Lafe Tarleton's face. From the deep mantel he brought a heavy family Bible and spread it before Jeremiah, opening to the pages on births, deaths, and marriages. There were the dates for Josiah Tarleton and his wife Lilith. There was the record of his mother's birth, her marriage to Seth Kincaid.

Arabella Tarleton, joined in holy wedlock to Seth Kincaid, on June 10 in the year of Our Lord, 1884.

Lafe himself must have written in Jeremiah's birth, for the letters were labored; the year 1893, but not the month and day, was given. It gave Jerry a sense of belonging to this room, to these books, and even to the bearded man he had always been taught to fear.

"Am I next of kin, Uncle Lafe?"

The man nodded.

"I ain't got ary a thing to remember my mam by," Jeremiah said, stroking the violin, but not intending to beg anything so precious as the fiddle.

There was a moment in which Lafe Tarleton might have given Jeremiah the beautiful instrument, but the moment passed as Jeremiah himself broke the spell.

How could he have forgotten his lost lamb all these hours? Overwhelmed with sorrow, and aware that darkness had fallen, he hurried into his clothes, now warm and dry. He wanted to go searching Danny even though it was night, but Lafe restrained him. Moonling or not, Tarleton knew that he must get Jeremiah down the valley to his pasture fence. He took no lantern, but led the boy with uncanny vision through the night. At last they saw Granny's faithful lantern coming through the dark and the high, frightened old voice crying, "Jeremiah, Jeremiah . . ."

"Coming, Granny."

"Lord in heaven. I thought you was daid and struck by lightnin'."

"Granny, Lafe found me, and . . ."

He turned to bring his new friend into the lamplight. But Lafe Tarleton had disappeared into the night as silently as a big cat. Granny didn't say a word, just buttoned her lip and looked her disapproval. Jerry wondered if he had dreamed of the firelight and the violin and the old family Bible. Maybe he had only dreamed that Lafe had promised to hunt for his lamb.

"I kin find Danny with the lantern."

"Yo're coming home to supper and to bed."

"Please, Granny."

"And a mustard plaster and maybe a good switchin'."

"But the dogs might get him."

"You heered me."

"Yes, Granny. I'm coming."

"Rain, rain, rain," said Uncle Hiram, wiping his feet on the doormat; "never seen so much rain since Noah built the ark."

"Come in, Hiram, and set by the fire; real unseasonable weather, ain't it?" Granny drew a shawl around her thin shoulders, shivering.

"Old bones is cold bones," Hiram admitted, looking at Samantha sharply. "I been aworryin' about you, Granny."

"Don't keer about myself," the tired woman said, putting another piece of hickory on the fire. "It's that boy-child I'm frettin' about. He ain't et a square meal the last three days."

"You fed him yarbs?"

142

"I fed him a passel of yarbs. I fed him sassyfras tea and catnip tea and sage tea. I fed him yellow dock, bitterroot, and spice bush. I doctored him with sulphur 'n' molasses and sugar 'n' kerosene, and I don't know what all."

"I reckon that should kill him or cure him," said Uncle Hiram, drawing up a settin' chair.

"It ain't yarbs he needs, Hiram."

"No," said Hiram, gazing thoughtfully into the fire. "It ain't yarbs."

"He's wastin' away for that lost lamb of hisn."

"He's a lost lamb his ownself," said Uncle Hiram sadly.

"Iffen we could only take his mind offen his troubles," said Granny, twisting the corner of her apron. "I'm at my wit's end, Hiram."

"I keep alookin' for the lamb," Hiram said. "'Tain't much use, I'm afraid. Them sheep-killin' dogs got him by this time, most likely."

"You keep alookin' and I'll keep adoctorin', and we'll both keep aprayin'," said Granny, "and in the Lord's good time he'll see it our way."

"Didn't tell you about goin' up to Lafe Tarleton's place," Hiram said. "Guess he's tetched in the haid all right."

"Lafe run you off the place with a shotgun?"

"Nooooo. Acted real neighborly. I asked him if he'd seen a black lamb. He nodded his head like crazy. Grabbed my arm and led me over to his sheep paddock."

"Glory be," Granny cried. "Glory hallelujah. Why didn't you tell me the lamb's safe?"

"Hold your horses, Samantha. Lamb ain't safe and never was, most likely."

"Well, say yore say and spite the devil," said Granny with exasperation.

"Went over to the paddock. Couldn't see hide nor hair of ary a black lamb."

"Jumped the fence, maybe."

"Purty high fence."

"Look for footprints?"

"Lafe did. Put on quite a show. Course the rain mighta washed 'em out." Hiram lit his pipe thoughtfully and tossed the match into the fire. "It's jest possible Lafe caught the lamb, put him in the paddock for safekeeping. Then maybe that old devil-ram of hisn seen this strange young buck sheep and chased him to hell and gone out of there."

"Could be."

" 'Tain't likely."

"No use gettin' the boy's hopes up," Granny said; "either way the lamb's still lost."

"Best not to tell him," Hiram agreed.

But it was a sorrowful thing to see Jeremiah lying in his bed, cheeks pale and drawn, pining for his lamb. Uncle Hiram had made him a slippery-elm whistle with a whole octave of notes. Jeremiah said, "Thank you kindly, Uncle Hiram," but did not try to blow it. Granny had made fresh doughnuts, always Jerry's favorite victual, but she could not tempt him. Sometimes he did not answer when she spoke to him, but lay rigid, staring at the rafters, his lips tight.

"Maybe you should call old Doc MacIntosh," Hiram said as he was leaving.

"Killed more folks than he ever cured," Samantha said scornfully. "What kin he do that I cain't?"

"Wal, take his pulse and temperature, for instance."

"I don't need no little glass tube to tell if Jeremiah has the fever. Any fool kin tell that by feelin' a person's forehead and seein' if his lips are cracked."

"Doc might give the boy some medicine."

"Pink pills ain't agoin' to cure lost-lamb sickness," Granny said; "only cure for that is findin' the lost lamb."

"I'll keep lookin'," Hiram promised, "but I'm losin' hope."

Daytimes were bad enough, but when the stormy nights came down upon Cat Hollow, Samantha was beside herself with worry. The lightning would flash through the loft window followed by the rumble of thunder and the wash of rain across the roof. And

Granny sitting there beside Jerry's bed in lamplight was at a loss to comfort him.

"I know it's a vexin' thing, a cruel thing. But maybe he's safe somewhar in a big old hollow log."

"You reckon he ain't dead?"

"Ain't saying he is and I ain't saying he ain't. But leastways he's in the hands of the Lord. And one way or the other we ain't agoin' to question the ways of the Almighty."

"I'll question His way," the boy whispered, "iffen He lets sheep-killin' dogs get my lamb."

"Jeremiah," Granny said sharply, "how dare you blaspheme the Holy Spirit?"

"Oh, Granny. He cain't, He cain't, He cain't kill my little black buck lamb."

"Didn't say He would," Granny comforted. "I only said, 'The Lord giveth and the Lord taketh away, blessed is the name of the Lord.'"

"If He takes my lamb . . ." Jeremiah began.

He was interrupted by a terrific flash of lightning and an earth-shaking explosion of thunder.

"Hear that, Jeremiah? That's the Lord God Almighty gettin' riled. You better say yore prayers and say 'em humble."

"He can't have my lamb," Jerry whispered, glaring past his granny into the storm beyond the window, into the very face of his tormentor.

Granny felt as though she had been slapped. It was a shocking thing to hear those words from Jeremiah's lips, a frightening thing to be there under the slanting roof, storm-bound and at God's mercy. But she feared more for Jerry than for herself. Squaring her thin shoulders in the lamplight, she said:

"Jeremiah Kincaid! You ask the Lord's forgiveness."

"No," Jerry whispered.

Granny shook her head in self-condemnation.

"It ain't his fault. O Lord, it's mine," she informed the Almighty. "I've tried to be mother and father to him, feed his soul and feed his body, but I reckon I've failed."

She hoped that Jeremiah would deny her words,

145

but he lay rigid and rebellious, hard in his heart as seasoned hickory.

"You've turned away from God," Granny said. "You've sassed yore Creator. It's one thing to blame poor Tildy for lettin' the lamb get away, or to blame yore uncle Hiram for not findin' it. But it's another thing entirely to raise up on yore hind legs and give back talk to yore Maker.

"You hear me, Jeremiah Kincaid?" (There was a note of panic in her voice which mingled with the wind crying at the eaves.) "Must the Lord smite you as he did Saul of Tarsus on the road to Jericho? Must you be blinded that you may see the light? You loved that lamb, and so I let you keep him. But lovin' a lamb more than you love God Almighty . . ."

"Love ain't wicked," Jerry said.

"No," Granny said, "love ain't wicked, unless you love yore ownself better than you love God."

"How kin I love God," Jerry asked, "when He took my mam and pap and now my lamb?"

It was a hard question to answer, and Samantha Kincaid was silent, seeking guidance. Except for the whisper of rain on the roof and the sputtering of the lamp wick, the only sound in the room was that of Jeremiah's heavy breathing. His face was hard as he stared wide-eyed at the rafters and beyond. Suddenly he began to shiver as with a chill and to ask for extra covers.

A sad thought struck Samantha as she descended to the great room to bring a cover. There, all complete and beautiful and new, lay "Cat Hollow Wedding" which was to be Jeremiah's Christmas present. But the boy might never live to see another Christmas. Better to give it now, when he needed its warmth. Snatching up the handsome coverlet, she mounted the ladder to the loft. Tenderly she spread it over him, tucking it in around the edges.

"I brung you a present, Jerry."

"Danny?" the boy said eagerly. "You found my lamb, Granny?"

"No," said Granny slowly, "jest this new Cat Hollow Wedding kiver."

"Oh, thank you kindly," the boy said. "That's a real nice present, Granny." But she could hear the disappointment in his voice, sorrowful as the unseasonable storm now raging around the cabin.

"I were savin' it for yore Christmas present."

"Onliest present I want," Jerry whispered, "is that little black buck lamb of mine."

Independent of his mind, Jeremiah's fingers began to trace the patterns of his new cover. Little by little his chill departed.

"Where's my mam and pap buried at, Granny?"

"Hush, child, I ain't finished my ballad song yet."

"Iffen I should die before I wake," Jeremiah said, using the words of the prayer he had steadfastly refused to say since the loss of his lamb, "it would be a sorry thing, not even knowing what become of my mam and pap."

"Got burned up in a stable fire," Granny said. "I were agoin' to break it to you gentle in a song ballad . . ."

"Where at?"

"Down in the bluegrass on a stormy night like this."

"What for did they go in a burnin' stable?"

"I fault yore mam for it," Granny said. "I allus figgered she sent yore pap into that flamin' barn jest to git rid of him."

"Was mam's race horse in that barn?"

"Course that was her excuse," Granny said.

"How did my mam get burnt?"

"Never could figger it out. Now go to sleep, child. It's gettin' late."

His head was filled with questions about that other stormy night. But stronger than his curiosity about his own parents was his wonder at the ways of the Almighty.

"Is God all-merciful?"

"Yes, Jeremiah."

"Is God all-powerful?"

"Yes, Jerry."

"He cain't be both. He jest cain't."

"Blasphemin' again," Samantha mourned.

" 'Cause if He's all-merciful He wouldn't burn up my mam and pap and kill my lamb."

"Maybe He couldn't do a thing about it."

"Then He ain't all-powerful," Jeremiah said fiercely. "Iffen He's all-powerful He can find my lamb right now. I dare Him!"

"It's the Lord's own mercy we ain't struck by lightnin'."

"I double-dare him!"

"Yo're a little kingbird fightin' an eagle," Granny said. "If you wasn't sick-a-bed I'd larrup you. I don't know where I've failed or what I kin do to make you see the light. Looks like it's up to you and yore Creator to thrash it out between you. Time'll come, however, when you know yo're wrong and He's right. Don't know how and don't know when. Maybe tonight in yore dreams you'll find the truth deep in yore own heart—with the help of Him yo're now blasphemin'."

Granny sighed and turned toward the ladder. Slowly and wearily she went to the room below. Taking her lamp and her Bible, she went into her bedroom, closing the door behind her.

As the winds of heaven can ruffle the surface of a pool, so the black winds of fear disturbed the spirit of Jeremiah. Above the roof tree the summer storm still raged, but in his fitful sleep Jeremiah believed it was already October. Picking up his dream where he had left it when Lafe Tarleton had rescued him from the flooded creek, he saw the wild autumnal sky filled with tossing white clouds like moiling sheep in a deep blue pasture.

Even as he watched, the woods turned gold and scarlet; sumac became the burning bush. Never before had he seen the wind so quickly strip the trees, until they stood bare-limbed and bleak against a desolate sky. Throughout this comfortless season of his dream he seemed to be combing the woods in desperate haste, seeking his lost lamb. Always he was followed by some enormous being, haunted by supernal but silent laughter, roughly handled by the sudden gales that whipped down the valleys. He followed creek beds high into the hills—but he was not alone.

And in this dream he came to cabin after cabin, approached identical doors with similar fear. Always the door was stealthily opened by the same rough-garbed, heavily bearded man. And always Jeremiah seemed small and almost voiceless as he whispered his question.

"Ary a black lamb, son," came the invariable answer.

"But you must have seen him."

"This critter yourn?"

"Raised him from an orphan on a bottle."

"Ain't seen hide nor hair," the bearded face would say, shaking with noiseless laughter.

Ice tingled along Jeremiah's spine as the cabin door closed, and closed and closed again, while autumn leaves whirled and hissed across the stoop.

Wearily he turned each time to start again his endless search through the hills, examining every frosty path for cloven hoofprints, scanning each bramble patch and fence for smidgins of black wool. It was ghostly to hear his own voice wailing through the hills, "Danny, Danny," over and over until it was merely a whisper, like that of the dry leaves frightened by the wind.

And the homecoming in this repetitious dream was always long after dusk-dark, with Granny waiting for him in the pasture, searching and crying and holding the light aloft. Even in his sleep Jeremiah somehow realized that Granny's search for him was like his search for the lamb. Yet at the lamplit table he seldom ate the food she had prepared or touched the steaming cup of sassafras tea she always offered.

After she had tucked him in bed with a hot brick wrapped in flannel, she would sit awhile trying to comfort him, saying:

"They's a passel of spring lambs out thar in the shed."

149

"Yes, Granny."

"One critter's as good as the next, I reckon."

"I reckon."

"Land of Goshen, child. There ain't one particle of use breakin' yore heart over a dumb brute-beast."

"Danny weren't any dumb brute-beast. He were human same as you and me, Granny."

"Sech a notion."

"Follered me everywhar. Butted his head against me like a little billy goat."

"Real mean and ornery. Jest like he should be."

"Reckon he got et by dogs?"

"He'd put up a tarnal good fight."

"Mighta got drownded or struck by lightnin' or . . ."

But at this point in his dream Granny always lost patience with him and said, "If he's daid he's daid. Now hush, and say yore prayers and go right off to sleep."

"Won't never say my prayers again."

"I'll have to switch you."

"Never again in all my born days, 'less God gives me back my lamb."

It was all mixed up in his dream: the many days of search, the many troubled nights in his loft bedroom, his often-repeated refusal to pray, the unprecedented week of storm. The elements had always before sounded friendly on the cabin roof. Now the wind snaked across the rooftop like a great black cat trying his claws on every loose shingle, whining at the chimney.

Sometimes he could not tell whether he was dreaming or awake; whether old Doc MacIntosh had climbed the loft ladder, or whether he imagined it. Often he must have cried out in his sleep, for suddenly lamplight would fill the room, and Granny's enormous, frightened shadow would sweep the rafters, while her voice would say:

"Jeremiah, speak to me! Lord in heaven, what have I done to deserve this affliction?"

"I'm all right, Granny."

"Ravin' like a lunatick."

"But you got to get Danny in the ark, he'll get drownded."

"Glory be, the pore child thinks it's Noah's flood. Thinks it's been rainin' forty days and forty nights."

"Save him, Granny. Save him."

"Ain't but one thing in the world'll save you *or* yore lamb."

"Tell me, Granny?"

"You gotter pray—and ask the Lord to forgive you, a pore little sinner."

"I ain't never agoin' to pray again. Not till he gives me back my lamb."

"You ain't alookin' for no lamb," Samantha Kincaid said in desperation. "Them cloven hoofprints yore alookin' for are the hoofprints of Satan hisself. He's acomin' to git you for blasphemin' the Lord."

And although Jeremiah trembled with a new chill and a new fear he refused to pray. For more than an hour Granny walked the floor, her shadow sweeping the rafters, while the wind outside tore at the shingles. But she could not induce the sick boy to pray.

And then the dream changed. The first snow was falling softly, and Uncle Hiram and Tildy and Jeremiah were in a cave-like recess in the rock. All around them were blocks of beautiful wood, and from a carpenter's kit Uncle Hiram was taking all the tools they needed to carve this wood into handsome, life-sized animals. The carving went ever so rapidly. Almost without effort Uncle Hiram was shaping a rosy-tinted calf from a block of wild cherry. A crowing rooster with his flock, a gay burro with large ears, plump pigs, and gentle cows were chiseled from the hard wood as if by magic.

And then the moment came to make the child for whom these creatures kneeled.

" 'Twern't no trick at all to carve the gentle beasts to watch over Him. But I reckon fashioning a Christ child for the Holy stable takes a reverent heart," said Uncle Hiram. "Here, you try it, Jerry."

But whereas all the native hardwoods of Pike County had melted before his tools while Jerry

151

helped carve the animals, the wise men, and even the angels, he could not scratch the surface of the beautifully grained wood from which he hoped to carve the baby Jesus.

Desperately Jeremiah tried to shape the wood, but not a chip would fly. The substance was as hard as his own heart.

"Not so all-fired rough," Uncle Hiram cautioned. "You kin only fashion Him through love." And when Uncle Hiram took up the task, lo and behold, the wood answered every suggestion of his tool. Before the wondering eyes of Jeremiah and Tildy the Christ child emerged, so real and so beautiful that they were silent with wonder. Faintly about the curls of the noble little head a strange light seemed to shine.

"You can help fix the cradle," Uncle Hiram said gently, and the children fell to work fitting and sanding to a satin finish the mountain cradle to hold the baby Jesus.

"It's a real purty cradle," Tildy said. "But in the Bible . . ."

"They lay the babe in a manger," Uncle Hiram concluded. "I know. But 'tain't the word of the Gospel so much as the spirit. Seems to like that cradle, don't He?"

"Any baby would," Tildy said, lifting the Christ child gently into the new golden straw.

Meanwhile in his heart Jeremiah was pondering the parable of the wood he could not carve, the block as hard as the cold inner core of his own being since he had lost his lamb. And Uncle Hiram, as though reading his thoughts, said:

"Try again, Jerry."

Still wondering greatly, and disturbed, Jeremiah chose a block of seasoned black walnut and began carving with consummate ease a black lamb for the Holy stable—a living, breathing, speaking likeness of Danny. He realized, with sudden joy, that here was a deathless image of his lamb as he would always remember him.

"You see," said Uncle Hiram, "it's easy to shape your lamb because you love him."

Those were somehow infinitely comforting words. For the first time in days and nights he seemed to be warm and unafraid. He turned to thank Uncle Hiram for the lesson he had taught. But he was alone in the cave with Mary and Joseph and the beautiful child, and the animals and the wise men and the angels.

He dreamed that it was the night before Christmas and he was lying in his bed in the loft under a star-of-Bethlehem cover with all the Nativity figures woven around the border. But although he himself was warm and he could hear Granny decorating the tree and arranging the presents she had made, he could think only of his lamb out in the snow and wind, half-frozen, trying to find his way home. He hoped that Granny still kept the light in the window as she had promised. Suddenly he was lonesome to be near her. He crawled across the floor to the loft hole and peered down.

She seemed so very far away, so small and tired and so lost to him he could have wept. But when she turned and saw him she cried cheerily:

"Fotch yore stockin', child."

"Yes, Granny."

"Land sakes, when I was yore age, no granny woman had to tell me to fotch my stockin'."

"I'm sorry, Granny."

She seemed to be floating toward him, growing bigger until her careworn face was close to his own. Great tears were trickling down her wrinkled cheeks.

"Ain't there anything in the whole world'll make you happy on Christmas morning? Ain't there some present yo're specially cravin'?"

"Yes," said Jerry. "There's one thing I'm cravin': that little black buck lamb of mine."

"There ain't nobody in creation 'cept the Lord God Almighty kin find that lost lamb," said Granny. "And I reckon He's plumb wore out with yore tarnal pestering. Now iffen you'd open that hard little heart of yourn and pray . . ."

Her voice became smaller and her figure diminished. Now she was far away from him again, fixing the tree.

"It's a right handsome tree," his voice said softly.

" 'Tain't nothin'," Granny said tearfully from a far distance.

"It's the purtiest tree I ever seed. And, Granny . . ."

"Yes, child?"

"I spent all my cash money."

"Land of Goshen," said Granny, dabbing her eyes on the hem of her balmoral petticoat, "all yore cash money?"

"For you and Uncle Hiram and Tildy. They're real nice presents."

In his dream it was still Christmas Eve. During lulls in the blizzard outside he could hear the mantel clock striking eleven-fifteen then eleven-thirty. Granny had long since gone to bed, and the great room below was silent save for the ticking of the clock.

He knew that he must leave his warm bed and make his way through the blizzard, so that when the clock struck the witchy hour of midnight—the moment when animals can talk—he could ask a desperately important question of a group of gentle beasts which in his mind's eye seemed to be kneeling about a cradle. It was not at all clear to him where these animals were to be found; he was not even certain why they would know where he could find his lost lamb. But these were chances he must take.

In his dream he did not remember rising and dressing in his warmest clothes, or slipping out into the stormy night with a lantern. He only knew that he was plunging through the blizzard, holding the enhaloed lantern ahead of him in the swirling flakes.

He seemed to be heading down the lane for the pasture, but the snowdrifts were so high they even covered the fences. Curiously enough, although he was totally lost and did not rightly know his destination, a power stronger than himself seemed to be luring him through the storm.

Floundering through drifts, he began at last to weary. He knew from stories he had read in his *Mc-*

154

Guffey's Reader that he must not stop to rest or he might freeze. More and more slowly he moved through the rising storm. And then, in his dream, he heard himself asking for help.

"Please, God. Not for myself, but for my lamb. I gotta find him. He'll die in this storm."

He realized, with wonder, that he had been praying, and that suddenly the last of the hatred had gone out of his heart; that he needed help and would be grateful for it.

"I don't care if we never get to the Pike County Fair, dear Lord. We don't care about blue ribbons. Jest help me, so I kin help my lamb, and I promise —I promise——"

But he didn't even want God to know what it was he was promising. Because promises are hard to keep. And if he broke his promise to the Almighty there would be a real reason for giving up hope of the life everlasting.

"You'll jest have to take my word for what I'm promisin'," Jeremiah said.

And at that moment the storm began to subside. And through a rift in the clouds Jeremiah could see one of the planets shining brightly far up Bean Blossom Creek. So he followed the star through the snowy woods to a cave which now seemed familiar. He had been there but recently with Hiram and Tildy.

The wind had quartered now, and only enough snow had been blown into the crèche to silver the hair of Joseph and Mary and gently powder the sleeping animals. The Christ child lay glistening as though stars had fallen upon him, and on the wings of the angels and the turbans of the wise men there gleamed a silver light.

And lo, there beyond the cradle itself was curled not the lamb he had carved, but in its place Danny himself. His deep black wool was a tangle of burs, his cinnamon leggings were caked with mire, but his body was still strong and warm and filled with life.

"Danny," Jeremiah cried, "yo're safe!"

Blinking in the lantern light, his eyes shining green-gold as they had on the night of his birth, Danny started up in fear. Then, hearing the voice of his master, he came to Jeremiah's arms. The lost sheep was found again. There would be great rejoicing.

But as the boy closed his arms around the lamb, the vision melted. The cave was empty. And Jeremiah awoke trembling in his bed beneath the rafters. Far away a cock was crowing in the cool, misty summer morning.

12 THE PROMISE

Granny Kincaid stirred restlessly in her bed. Long years of rising with the birds made it difficult for her to steal extra winks of sleep after first cock's crow. Besides, it was purely sinful to lie abed like a hussy. She prided herself that winter or summer, rain or shine, breakfast was always on the table by six in the morning.

She did not wish to wake Jeremiah if he were still sleeping, so she took special care not to bang the stove lids as she started a chip fire for frying the bacon. Heaven be praised, the storm had finally ceased and the summer morning was cool and clear; but there was no answering sunshine in her heart as she contemplated the burden of sorrow that a lost lamb and a prideful young'un can bring to a cabin in the hills.

Half an hour later she mounted the ladder to the loft to see if Jerry were awake and if she could bring him a tempting breakfast. But the bed was empty and the boy's clothes were gone from their oaken peg.

She had a moment of terror remembering how Jeremiah had been blaspheming the Lord.

"No, 'tain't likely," she comforted herself; "iffen Satan come to fotch him, he wouldn't had time to put on his britches."

But the other alternative was frightening enough. He was doubtless wandering through the woods weary and wan and half out of his mind, still searching that lost lamb of his. The creek was so flooded by the rains he might fall in and drown. She hurried to the room below, untied her apron, slapped on her slat bonnet, and was rushing out the door when she heard the sound of hoofs on the gravel. A moment later Hiram was dismounting from his tired, mudstained horse.

"Been combing the countryside for that lamb. How's the boy?"

"Boy's gone, lamb's gone, and I reckon my patience is about gone too."

"Hmmm, hmmm," Hiram said. "Got right up out of his sickbed to hunt for Danny. I'll say one thing. Him and Tildy are *that* determined."

"Tildy?"

"She's out ahuntin' the lamb too. I suppose, soon as the storm let up, her maw had to say 'Yes.' Saw her about sunup, jest a patch of red gingham climbing the ridge. She figures she let the lamb out, and she's agoin' to get it back in the pen."

"Poor forlorn little critters." Granny sighed. "Three lost lambs."

"Don't know what to do with lamb or boy," Granny said. "I've tried bein' firm and I've tried bein' kind. I've tongue-lashed Jeremiah and I've cried over him. I've scolded and coaxed, fed him yarbs, and read him Scripture. He's hard as granite in that young heart of hisn."

"Can't expect an unshod colt to pull steady as an old horse. Give him time, Samantha, give him time. And give him enough rope."

"Said the same about my own son. Gave him too much time and too much rope . . ."

"You're still aprayin', I suppose?"

"Wore dents in the floorboards aside my bed."

"Lord ain't helpin' much, is He?"

"He certainly ain't. I got real sharp with Him last night, same as I do with you and Jerry."

"Might as well speak up in meetin'," Hiram agreed.

"Always pride myself that I speak my mind."

"It would have pleasured me to hear it. What all did you tell the Lord, Samantha?"

"I says, 'Lord, I'm about wore out with the way yo're messin' up our lives down here in Cat Hollow. I'm gettin' old and I'm gettin' tired. You tuk my David and you tuk my Seth, and it looks like yo're afixin' to take my Jeremiah. I'm a God-fearin', hard-workin', Christian woman, and you been asmitin' me and apesterin' me till you jest about broke my old heart.' "

"Amen," said Hiram. "What else did you tell Him, Samantha?"

"I says right out, 'I ain't askin' you, Lord; I'm atellin' you. Tetch that young'un's heart. Shew him the light that he may be saved. And iffen you got a mite of mercy, find that little lost black lamb of hisn.' "

"That was tellin' Him, Samantha."

"Hiram, I ain't a heathen, back-slidin' woman, you know that. I'm stanch in the faith; I'm aclimbin' slowly up the straight and narrer toward the pearly gates. But I'm afeared that iffen God don't answer one of my prayers pretty soon I'll misdoubt He ever *does* answer prayers."

"I've misdoubted it many a year," said Uncle Hiram quietly. "Mostly prayin' is just lettin' God know how you feel about things. Lettin' him share the burden that's on your mind."

"Howsomever," Samantha said, "after gettin' up off my aching old knees, I clumb into bed and dropped right off to sleep and had real pleasant dreams for a change. I sorta figured God had took over and decided to do the worryin' for a while."

"And then you woke up and found the boy was gone," Hiram prompted.

"It's enough to shake the faith of the twelve disciples," Samantha mourned.

Just then from far away came a small happy voice, crying, "He's safe. Jerry found him."

"That's Tildy, ain't it?" Granny asked.

"Sounds like her voice."

"He's found him, he's found him." Breathless and glowing, the small girl came racing up the lane bearing the good tidings. Now they could see Jerry and the lamb coming more slowly from the far edge of the pasture, skirting the widened creek.

"Must have been a guardian angel," Hiram said.

"We've been needin' one."

"Looks like prayer is answered now and then."

Granny Kincaid was too filled with emotion to answer. She merely glanced gratefully heavenward as girl, boy, and lamb came up the long lane.

"Don't seem much the worse for wear at this distance."

"Sorta wet and bedraggled," Granny said, "but alive and kickin'."

"You figure on takin' them to the fair, Granny?"

"I reckon. I'm that grateful to the Almighty."

Tildy opened the gate, and in another moment children and lamb were coming around the corner of the barn. They were babbling happily about getting Danny a meal of good warm mash; of combing the burs out of his wool. They were petting him and laughing over him and calling him endearing names, then scolding him lovingly for running away to the hills.

"I found him, Granny," Jerry said. "I had a dream."

"Where *did* you find him, son?"

"In a manger, like in Bethlehem," the boy said, with a strange, faraway light in his eyes. "I mean . . ."

Uncle Hiram gave Granny a swift puzzled look.

"I mean in that old cave up the creek in the Tarleton woods."

"How in the name of Glory . . . ?" Granny began.

"I told you. I had a dream. And, Uncle Hiram?"

"Yes, son."

"Kin you carve beautiful animals and wise men and angels and maybe even a baby Jesus for a crèche?"

160

"That's a real big job," Hiram said, "but we might try."

"Glory be," said Granny; "allus did say the Almighty answered prayer. You jest gotta know how to handle Him, that's all."

As the children hurried the lamb off to his pen, Hiram said to Samantha:

"I can pick up the tickets tomorrow. And I already got a box for your covers and a crate for the lamb —that is, if it's all right with you."

Samantha followed the children with her eyes, then heaved a long sigh of relief and resignation. "Land of Goodness, there's a sight of things to be done. We ain't got half our wearin' clothes yet."

"You reckon the boy should have a pair of store-bought britches?" Uncle Hiram asked delicately.

"Store-bought britches one day," Granny said sharply, "highfalutin notions the next. Many a young man has gone to hell 'cause his mam started him out in store-bought britches. Homespun's good enough for any Kincaid."

"No hard feelin's, Samantha. I jest thought you'd want him to look his best among all them outlanders."

"I reckon," Granny said, a dreamy look coming into her eyes. "And while we're squanderin' our cash money I might as well take off my slat bonnet and linsey-woolsey and get me a store-bought hat with a pretty on it and a black bombazine—no, maybe even a changeable silk. Lord in heaven, it's purely sinful, but I've always wanted an umbrella."

"Samantha," said Hiram, "you'll be the belle of the Pike County Fair."

"Cain't abide the thought of scornful outlanders asneerin' at our clothes. Gotta hold up our heads, don't we?"

"Tune up your fiddles," said Uncle Hiram. "Here comes the pride of Cat Hollow, dressed fit to kill."

"It's a good thing I knit me them new black mitts."

"Umm, umm," said Uncle Hiram. "What shockin' high-heeled notions. A new hat with a pretty, a change-

161

able silk dress, black mitts, and a purely sinful umbrella."

"It's a turrible temptation," Granny said with a happy sigh.

But as though no dream could last for long in Cat Hollow, Tildy now came running from the pen, wailing as though her heart would break, her face all tear-streaked and woe-begone.

"Why, what's the matter, baby?" Uncle Hiram asked.

"We're not agoin' to the fair."

"Huh, what's that?"

"He said—he—wasn't—agoin' to the fair."

"Like to know why not?" Granny bridled.

"He jest said ' 'cause.' "

Uncle Hiram cocked an eyebrow and exchanged a puzzled glance with Granny. Then he pulled Tildy to him and tried to comfort her, wiping away her tears with a big, clean bandanna handkerchief.

Wonderment and gentle determination struggled for possession of Samantha's face. She started toward the pen, followed by the others. Jerry was pouring mash into the feeding trough. He looked up as they entered.

"He's got enough burs in him," Granny said, removing a cluster of burdock.

"Yes'm, but he ain't got hardly a scratch on him."

"What you want to make Tildy cry for?"

"I told her she could go to the fair—and you—and Uncle Hiram." Jerry averted his face, brushing away a large unwanted tear.

"You and Danny ain't figgerin' on goin'?"

Jerry shook his head. "Changed our mind."

Samantha Kincaid put a gentle hand under the boy's chin, turning his face upward so that she could look into his eyes.

"What for did you change your mind, Jeremiah?"

"Made a secret promise—to God."

"What kind of a promise, son?"

"Promised God iffen He'd let me find my lamb, I wouldn't *take* him to the fair, and," Jerry added, his face breaking into a sunny smile, "He let me find him."

Jeremiah put his arm protectively around the lamb's neck. "Danny and I don't want no blue ribbons. We just want each other."

"Wal," said Granny, "wal, now. If this ain't a fine how-de-do."

Jerry looked questioningly at his grandmother.

"Happens I—that is," Granny faltered, "happens I made a promise too. Promised God if you *did* find yore lamb we *would* go to the fair."

Jeremiah stared with shock and joyous disbelief. The whole situation was much too complicated and wonderful for comprehension. Slowly his face began to light with ecstasy.

"And," Granny added firmly, "since I've known God fifty-one years longer than you have, I reckon He'll be expectin' *me* to keep *my* promise."

Jeremiah threw his arms around his granny and gave her weather-beaten face a loving kiss, tasting the salt of tears upon it. Samantha straightened up quite suddenly.

"Run fotch the currycombs, Jerry. There's a sight of burs in Danny's wool."

As Jerry and Tildy ran happily to do as they were bidden, Granny and Uncle Hiram exchanged a meaningful look. Then, turning away, Granny raised her eyes toward the bright morning sky.

"Forgive me, Lord," she said, "and thank you kindly."

13   PUTTING ON THE STYLE

Dressed in spang new wearing clothes, all duded up like outlanders, were Tildy, Hiram, and the Kincaids on that bright morning. Stiff-starch proud in their Sunday-go-to-meeting finery, but shy as woods mice in that elegant day coach (where the plush seats were as green as moss on a fallen log and only prickled a little under your knees).

It was a once-in-a-lifetime occasion, and it took more than ordinary courage to climb the train steps into the cars. Samantha clutched the arm of her seat and held her breath as Highball Johnson gave Old 99 the steam and slowly advanced the throttle. She had a moment of panic in which she spoke a quick and silent prayer, thinking her mortal time had come; but she was bound and determined not to let the others see her fear.

Once the train was rolling the panic left her and she felt airy as a swallow in swift flight. It was purely a pleasure to lean back in her seat and absorb the wonders of that car: the bright brass kerosene lamps with floral shades gently swinging from the ceiling;

the varnished woodwork; and far down the car the place where you could get a drink without cranking up a well bucket or working a pump handle.

"Cain't hardly believe it," said Granny Kincaid. "Hiram jest turned that leetle spigot and the water squirted out."

She wished that all the folks in Fulton Corners could see them now, "asittin' like quality and chawin' crackerjack." She agreed with Ecclesiastes that "Vanity of vanities; all is vanity." But just a little vanity is balm of Gilead to the spirit. It did her old eyes good to see Jeremiah in that new Norfolk suit with patch pockets and buttons at the knee. His copper-toed boots shone as brightly as his new bow tie and his well-scrubbed face—a handsome young'un if she-did-say-it-who-shouldn't.

Tildy was like an old-fashioned flower garden. Her straw hat, tied under her chin with a velvet ribbon, was abloom with forget-me-nots and talisman rosebuds.

"Yore maw surely done herself proud on that fair-goin' dress," Granny said; "never seed sech purty flowered voile, with puff sleeves and a pink sash and all."

"I got new underpants too," Tildy whispered to Granny, "and a new garter waist, and new petticoats —three of 'em."

"Hope it don't go to yore head," said Granny. But Samantha was in no moral position to upbraid anyone for primping and preening. She felt like a shameless hussy in her new, flat black straw dripping with purple grapes. Never in her life had she hoped to own a striped changeable silk dress with leg-of-mutton sleeves set off to a fare-thee-well by black mitts, black shawl, black umbrella, and new plush carryall.

"Dear Lord," she whispered happily to her Creator, "I'm a proud and sinful woman. But I wisht David could see me just once in all these wearin' clothes."

Uncle Hiram topped the whole kit and caboodle in his checked suit, white waistcoat, and stiff collar. Three ten-cent cigars with gilded bands peeped jauntily from his vest pocket, and his patent-leather button shoes were as dazzling as mirrors in the sunlight.

"You better behave yoreself in Midlothian," Samantha said sharply. "With all them city females."

Uncle Hiram snapped his galluses with his thumbs and smiled with self-satisfaction. "Gettin' jealous already, ain't you, Samantha?"

Jeremiah and Tildy had often watched the train go by and had dreamed of riding on the cars. But the reality was beyond all expectation.

"Look at them telephone poles, Tildy! They're agoin' backwards."

"That's 'cause we're agoin' frontwards," Tildy said. And then they both laughed and laughed for no good reason at all.

They invented a game. A haystack counted one, a red barn two, and a white horse five. It was a noisy game, and sometimes they argued about who saw it first.

But mostly they chattered about Danny in the baggage coach ahead. Since his miraculous rescue they had petted and pampered him almost to death. With Uncle Hiram's help they had scrubbed him clean in the creek, dried him in the sun, and combed and brushed his wool until it shimmered in the sunlight. His hoofs and horns were sandpapered to a satin finish and burnished with an oiled cloth. Then, to the children's dismay, Uncle Hiram had brought forth his clippers.

"You ain't agoin' to cl'p him, are you?" Jerry asked.

"The judges won't fancy a clipped lamb," Tildy added doubtfully.

"You jest trust your uncle Hiram. There's a lot of tricks to this trade."

"Don't hurt him," Tild' pleaded.

"I ain't agoin' to hurt him. And I ain't agoin' to shear him."

The children watched with concern as Hiram carefully trimmed the longest wool from the back.

"Looks like yo're makin' him square as a box," Jerry said.

"Blockin', they call it."

"What for do you block him?" Tildy wondered.

"Makes a critter look broad acrost the back."

"He's goin' to be awful purty," Tildy said for the hundredth time.

"Purty is as purty does," Hiram warned; "sometimes purty ain't enough."

But nothing could dampen the hopes of Jeremiah and Tildy now that the lamb was safe and the fairgoing journey assured. Already they were forgetting the days of terror when the lamb had been lost in the wilderness. Their hours were filled with coaxing and coaching, feeding and fussing over the frisky creature on whom all their hopes were pinned. If love and care could produce a winner, Danny's chances should have been excellent.

Even Granny had to admit he was a handsome little devil. "Happen he don't butt the jedges clean over the fence he orter take the consolation prize."

And once again both Hiram and Samantha warned that nothing was certain in this vale of tears, least of all the blue ribbon and the cash award.

"Pride . . ." began Granny.

"Goeth before destruction," Uncle Hiram concluded.

"We ain't afeared," Jeremiah said.

Deep in his heart the boy had reasoned that if the Lord God Almighty had watched over the lamb throughout the darkness and storm, had sent him a vision to help him rescue his pet, there was a well-laid plan behind this mercy. Like as not the Lord had figured out every last detail months in advance, from the moment He saw Jeremiah fall in love with the small black orphan. Now that he was back on speaking terms with the Almighty, Jeremiah kneeled down in his nightshirt every evening.

"Bless Granny, bless Uncle Hiram, bless Tildy—and let Danny win the blue ribbon! Please, God. Amen!"

The car wheels went clickety-clack, clickety-clack along the rails. Up ahead Old 99 wailed four times for every crossing and rang its deep-toned bell. Whoos! . they had crossed a river bridge with a fine hollow thunder. Farmers waved. Colts and calves in pasture high-tailed in wide-nostriled excitement.

It was better than riding on a magic carpet. And every moment there were new things to see.

Finally the conductor cried:

"Next stop Midlothian. Don't forget your parcels."

Tildy and Jeremiah could scarcely wait for the train to grind to a stop. Before the conductor could place his box below the step they jumped to the station platform. Samantha Kincaid, nimble as a nanny goat, needed no help to get down the steps. However, she quickly observed how the fine outland ladies let the conductor take their elbows. So when the blue-coated trainman offered to aid her, saying, "Watch your step, Granny," she accepted the surprising chivalry.

"Much obliged for the helpin' hand," she said.

Uncle Hiram ambled down, puffing his newly lit cigar, as proud and careless as though train rides happened every day. Granny was afraid the trip had already gone to his head. But she had no time to worry about Hiram, for a new and startling distraction was at hand.

A boy rushed up to help them with their luggage and nearly succeeded in snatching Granny's big carpetbag from her strong old hand.

"Not so tarnation fast, young feller," Granny said suspiciously.

"I just wanted to help you with the bag, ma'am."

"I fotched and carried afore yore pappy wore britches," said Granny Kincaid. "I'll tote my own, I reckon, or give it to that big lazy feller I brung along from Fulton Corners."

Uncle Hiram grinned sheepishly. He picked up Samantha's bag and his own, saying, "He didn't mean any harm, Granny."

"Cain't tell about these city slickers," said Granny Kincaid. "Like as not that torn-down scoundrel was afixin' to snatch that bag and high-tail for the tall timber."

Granny wasn't going to let any outlander get the better of her. She was in one of her managing moods, sharp as a fox and on tiptoe with excitement. So while the children drank from the first drinking fountain they had ever seen in their lives and fed pigeons cracker-jack, Uncle Hiram let Granny wrangle with a jolt-wagon driver who was waiting at the baggage platform where the lamb and quilts had been unloaded from the train. Hiram concluded that the more she tongue-larruped the driver, the less she'd argue with *him*.

The sad old owl on the wagon seat wanted half a dollar to take the lamb and quilts to the fairgrounds. Samantha said it was a sin and a shame, pure highway robbery. One way and another she beat him down until he said he'd settle for twenty-five cents. It was all Uncle Hiram could do to keep from laughing aloud to hear her.

"Lady," said the driver mournfully, "you plumb wore me down."

"Yo're a thievin' rascal," said Granny, as Hiram reached in his pocket for the quarter, "and we ain't takin' any chances. We're aridin' along."

"Most usually," said the driver, "I charge extra for passengers."

"Wait, Hiram," said Granny, restraining his hand, "hang onto that quarter."

"Oh, all right," said the driver in exasperation, "climb aboard. I can't lose any more than I'm losin' already."

Samantha and Hiram squeezed into the jolt-wagon seat with the driver. Jeremiah and Tildy stood behind them in the wagon box, holding onto the iron rail on the back of the seat. Cat Hollow saw Main Street in style, feeling sinfully extravagant. Miracle after miracle flashed by: three-story brick buildings rising majestically toward the treetops; town belles dressed like calendar pictures with cherries and roses on their hats and graceful skirts sweeping the board sidewalks; store windows filled with the fanciest bolt goods and finery this side of Indianapolis.

It was almost too wonderful for comprehension.

They were speechless with awe and admiration. Even Uncle Hiram was bug-eyed and silent, puffing rapidly on his expensive cigar. As they passed the first National Bank with its gilt lettering and white pillars their hearts were beating faster than the clop-clop of the horses' hoofs. Shy as a hollow log full of raccoon kits (and as curious), the delegation from Fulton Corners drank in the unsuspected beauties of this surprising new world. Their faces glowed with charmed astonishment. And for one fleeting moment Samantha wished that she had been born a fine lady in a metropolis like Midlothian and could have lived in a house with a cupola and a cast-iron deer in the front yard. She was so deep in her mood of wonder and wishful thinking that she did not see Hiram nod with pleasure at an old acquaintance (leaning against a lamppost, twirling a rabbit's foot on his gold watch chain with cosmopolitan *savoir-faire*). It was perhaps fortunate for Hiram that everyone's attention in the next few moments was captured by a terrifying spectacle.

Down the street, cut loose from its horses, and making a commotion that would scare the living daylights out of John L. Sullivan himself, came a bright red contrivance raising a great cloud of dust.

"What's that there thing?" Granny shouted. "Jump—jump for yore lives."

"It's jest an auto*mo*bile," said Hiram soothingly.

"Heavens-to-Betsy," Granny shouted, "it's acomin' right at us."

"Gee, what a beauty," Jerry cried.

"I'm scared," Tildy said.

"Whoa, boys," said the driver. "Easy, now."

The horses trembled and shied. They reared and whinnied. The driver held the reins firmly and prepared for the worst. At the last moment Tildy covered her eyes, but she peeked out from between her fingers. Breathing fire from its exhaust, burping its horn and grinding its gears, the horseless carriage came roaring past. The driver and his passengers looked scarcely human in their goggles, caps, and white dusters.

"Them gol-darned contraptions," said the driver.

170

"Excusin' my swearin', ma'am, there should oughta be a law agin 'em. I'd like to meet up with this feller Henry Ford. I'd give him a piece of my mind."

After such a narrow escape from death shared by all in the jolt wagon, everyone felt warm and friendly.

"My name's Gus," said the driver. "Gloomy Gus some folks call me."

"My name's Tildy."

"Mine's Jerry, and this is my granny."

"Mine's Hiram Douglas."

"Pleased to meetcha," said Gus. "On the right you see the Pike County Courthouse."

"Golly," said Jerry, "I'll bet that's bigger than the state capitol."

"Or the national capitol in Washington, maybe," Tildy added.

"It musta cost a right smart passel of money," said Granny Kincaid.

"More than one hundred thousand dollars," said Gloomy Gus with sorrowful pride.

"Wheeww!" said Uncle Hiram, forgetting his secret promise not to be too impressed by anything.

A moment later, and for no apparent reason, their new friend began to sing in what had once been a barbershop baritone voice:

"Young man in a carriage drivin' like he's mad
With a team of horses borrowed from his dad;
Cracks his whip so lively to make his lady smile.
Course we know he's only puttin' on the style."

As though to fit his action to his song, Gus urged his old team into a smart trot. Samantha's foot had already started to beat the time against the low dashboard. The horses were listening. You could tell it by the way they picked up their big pantalooned feet. Jerry and Tildy, standing in the wagon box, began sashaying a bit from side to side. Uncle Hiram, not to be outdone, took a mouth organ from his pocket and after a practice run began tonguing the tune like a steam calliope.

171

"That's a tyrolickin' ballad song if I ever heered one," said Granny pleasantly.

"Want to hear the chorus?"

"Baaa," said Danny, thrusting his woolly black head through the wide slats of the crate.

"We'd be much obliged," said Jerry seriously. "And you mustn't pay Danny no mind. He's forgotten his manners."

Gloomy Gus threw back his head and rolled out the chorus while beating time with the butt of his whip:

"Puttin' on the agony, puttin' on the style,
That's what all the young folks are doing all the while.
When I look around me I'm very apt to smile
To see so many people puttin' on the style."

There were many verses concerning a young man home from college who used words that couldn't be found in Webster; a sweet young miss who went to church just to see the boys, and many another young character who needed putting in his place for "Putting on the Style." And by that time Samantha and Uncle Hiram were making up verses to fit the occasion.

"Country lads and lasses going to the fair,
Ferris wheels to whirl them high up in the air;
Plunkin' down their nickels, squanderin' a pile,
Eatin' cotton candy, puttin' on the style."

As the jolt wagon whirled into the fairgrounds and past the merry-go-round, Uncle Hiram topped all the previous verses:

"Ride a wooden filly, never leaves the track,
Feller says it's silly. All you git is back;
Really don't go nowhar, costs a dime a mile,
Canterin' in circles, puttin' on the style . . ."

Hiram might have done better with his impromptu versifying. But his mind was on a very different matter. If Tuck Goodspeed were still alive and whirling his rabbit foot there was no time to be wasted.

14 THE PIKE COUNTY FAIR

Not since Samantha Kincaid's great-grand-mother had come through the Cumberland Gap and up the wilderness trails to Kentucky's dark and bloody ground had any member of her immediate family set eyes upon such a spectacle as the Pike County Fair. Castles and great houses were mentioned in the ballads (remembered from the far away and long ago). But surely they could not have been more beautiful than the white fair buildings with their green roofs in the oak opening to the north of Midlothian. Brave young lairds rode prancing steeds in many of the old songs. But were ever man and horse more skillfully blended than the jockeys in their bright silks urging their sleek mounts around the smooth oval before the pennanted pavilion?

There was a girl as handsome as Fair Ellen, risking her neck in a death-defying act, dancing on a tight wire with a pink umbrella. And there was a devil in human form who swallowed fire, lay on a bed of spikes, and walked barefooted over glowing coals.

In the livestock buildings, the big Percheron and Belgian horses, gentle Jersey and Guernsey cows, Poland China, Duroc, and Hampshire hogs were all better fed than any man, woman, or child in Cat Hollow. The horses had bright ribbons braided into their manes and tails. They were curried until they shone like milkweed silk.

Cat Hollow pigs were lean and wild, but these proud creatures were round as butterballs and clean as a hound's tooth. Their tails were curled in perpetual question marks asking "When do we eat?"

Whereas old Blueberry, the Kincaid family cow, had a crumpled horn, one wall eye, and a back that sagged (like the barn roof over her head), these pure-bred island cattle had all the points of aristocratic cowdom. Proud owners talked, in a jargon all their own, of blood lines and pedigrees and butter-fat production.

But you had to watch your cash money at the County Fair. It looked easy enough to toss rings over Kewpie dolls, guess which shell hid the pea, or (Hiram thought) swing the sixteen-pound sledge and ring the bell. Usually, however, you lost your nickel. Samantha said that if Uncle Hiram wanted to throw away his money on such sinful nonsense, that was his own affair. But she added that it wasn't fitting nor decent nor Christian to teach young'uns to gamble, much less to see half-naked women tattooed with fancy pictures. She told the sideshow barker a thing or two when the World's Smallest Baby turned out to be a chattering little monkey, and the two-headed calf was not only dead and stuffed but moth-eaten in the bargain. But she loved the Ferris wheel; quickly acquired a taste for lemon pop, and risked eternal damnation by winning first an antimacassar and next a gilt-framed "God Bless Our Happy Home" by threading three needles in less than a minute. The needle-threading concessionaire complained that Samantha would run him out of business.

174

" 'Tweren't really gamblin', were it?" Granny defended herself.

"Don't know what else you could call it," Hiram insisted.

"Cain't call a sure thing like threadin' a needle gamblin'."

"You're a sinful old woman," Hiram said, "and you're lovin' it."

After Hiram had helped Granny arrange her covers and had seen Danny safely into his pen, he disappeared on some mysterious mission of his own. Both children were as fresh as daisies, so Granny let them go exploring while she rested her bones, sitting beside her display with an ear cocked for compliments.

She wished that she might write a ballad about the Great Pike County Fair so that even Jeremiah's and Tildy's grandchildren would have some way to know how beautiful it had been. It was a sorrowful thing how quickly such a moment might pass, and with it all the wonder and mystery, the laughter and shouting, the music of the merry-go-round. All these would fade unless she could capture them in a ballad to sing through the years beside the fire in her Cat Hollow cabin.

Most of all, she wanted her verses to reveal the excitement of the quilt and coverlet contest:

> " 'Twere a sight to see the kivers
> At the Pike County Fair;
> All the weavers in Pike County
> Fotched their counterpanes there!"

The Midlothian Ladies' Aid had entered a quilt called "Beautiful Ohio," one of the prettiest patterns Granny had ever seen. Each little octagon of silk was cut as carefully as a jewel, and the stitches were so fine you could scarcely see them without a reading glass. By using two shades of blue for the water, the Midlothian women had achieved an effect of small waves dancing in the sunshine.

"That's real nice quiltin'," the lady judges admitted,

175

rustling up in their black bombazine dresses for a closer inspection. "All them purty steamboats on that bright blue river."

> "The Ladies' Aid was prideful
> Of their highfalutin kiver
> With a right smart o' steamboats
> On an indigo river!"

A gentle old man with a long white beard from far up Indian Creek entered "Star of the East," a coverlet in many shades of yellow, sparkling as a pasture of dandelions in the spring. Samantha had to admit that old Uncle Ebenezer Overholt could weave like a Baltimore oriole. He could handle "Summer and Winter Weave," "Double Weave," and "Overshot Weave" better than most womenfolk,

> "And Uncle Ebenezer
> Used a yaller that was yaller,
> From Black-eyed Susan blossoms
> Plucked at sunup in some holler."

Yes, Uncle Ebenezer, with his snowy beard and bright blue eyes, was a favorite with the judges. He might prove to be serious competition.

But Samantha Kincaid had bethought her to bring along samples of her dyes and some of the flowers and roots and berries from which they were extracted. In more than a dozen little jam pots were the tempered reds she had used, the mellow yellows, and the soft blues. Sealed in pint mason jars were the substances from which these colors came: madder and sumac bobs for her reds, bog myrtle from which she made her best yellow; privet leaves, apple bark, and touch-me-not ranging from dull brass to bright gold. No woman could pass up such an exhibit. It excited the judges even before they began to examine her exquisitely woven coverlets.

"That's a real nice 'Chips and Whetstones,' " one of the judges said.

"Thank you kindly," Granny murmured.

"What do you call that story cover?"

"Cat Hollow Wedding."

The judges went into a sibilant huddle, examined the coverlet again, made notes, pointed with shocked surprise at the unmistakable little horns showing from the curly hair of the preacher joining the pair in holy wedlock, puzzled over the curious symbols leading from the altar to the grave.

"I preached me a sermon in that kiver," Granny explained. "And I sung me a psalm."

As the judges moved on to other contestants, Samantha suddenly realized that there was no longer much bitterness in her heart about Seth and Arabella. Somehow the sermon on her counterpane had become a song of quiet sorrow. She was almost ready to let bygones be bygones. She wished that she might somewhere find evidence that would help her to forgive the fiddling woman and thus lay her saucy and sinful ghost.

For although Granny had never really given her blessing to the wedding commemorated on the story cover, she was now asking the Almighty for a second chance. The way Samantha figured it, she was now being tested and tried before the Judgment Seat. If the Lord had helped her weave the most beautiful counterpane at the Pike County Fair around a theme which had been gall and wormwood to her spirit, then surely it was a sign that the Lord had forgiven her as *she* must forgive Arabella. She was so deep in her thoughts she scarcely noticed the return visit of the judges. But looking up, she saw the blue ribbon being pinned to the counterpane. Possibly it was an accident that the lower tip of the ribbon modestly covered the preacher's horns. Samantha felt no affront at this gentle criticism; maybe she shouldn't have woven that detail into the pattern in the first place.

> *"Oh, the jedges kept alookin'*
> *At Cat Hollow Weddin',*
> *Said they'd never seen the like*
> *In hand-wove beddin'.*

177

> *"Let the red rose and the white rose*
> *Intertwine the bridal pair,*
> *For Granny took the ribbon*
> *At the Pike County Fair."*

After the judges had congratulated her, a small crowd of women gathered asking Samantha about her wool and dyes. Granny was flattered, but she was watchful. She didn't completely trust all this new-found warmth among the outlanders. A mauve-enswathed matron offered fifty dollars for her prize-winning coverlet.

"Never seed fifty cash dollars in all my born days," Granny admitted honestly.

"Then, of course, you'll be willing to sell," said the banker's wife, reaching into her handbag.

"Lady, my kivers ain't for sale."

"But, my good woman, why not? You need the money."

"My kivers pleasure me, that's why not," said Granny firmly. "And cash money ain't everything."

But Samantha would have sold her prize coverlet; she would have given away her blue ribbon; she would have offered anything she had on earth if she could have altered what she was certain would be the defeat of Danny and Jeremiah in the lamb-judging contest.

In the sheep pavilion, Granny's instinct told her more strongly than ever that this was indeed Judgment Day. On this day the Lord would come to judge the quick and the dead.

The clear voice of the announcer shouting through his megaphone might very well have been Gabriel's (for the judging of the spring rams was at hand).

In the pens adjoining the arena, men and boys were giving final beauty treatments to their animals. The jury of three good men and true were taking a preliminary survey of the field, feeling the fleeces for fineness, looking at hoofs and teeth and horns. They cocked their heads, looking as wise as Solomon, and made mysterious marks in little notebooks; talked knowingly of the long-wool breeds and the fine-wool breeds—the Cotswolds and the Lincolns; the Merinos and the Rambouillets. Jeremiah and Tildy realized sadly that they didn't understand more than half of the learned talk which came to their ears, and neither did Samantha Kincaid.

"The old goats," sniffed Granny. "I cain't hardly tell 'em from the critters they're jedgin'. And where in tarnation is Hiram, you s'pose? I told him to get back here in plenty of time with that neat's-foot oil."

Down in the straw in her very best dress, Granny was helping the children snip stray wisps of wool from Danny's back. She wanted the oil for a last polish of hoofs and horns. And they all needed Hiram's calm self-assurance. Samantha's heart was as full as Bean Blossom Creek in April with hope and fear and love for the boy and his lamb—so, of course, she was particularly sharp with everyone.

"Off gambling again, most likely; wastin' his nickels throwin' rings. Cain't trust nobody nowadays. Shouldn't have let him get out of my sight. Shoulda gone for that neat's-foot oil my ownself."

"Granny, I feel . . ."

"How do you feel, son?"

"Like jest before we found the bee tree, Granny. Like jest before I found Danny in the cave. . . ."

"All spring rams in the arena at once, please."

"Like on the Day of Judgment," Granny said, a feeling of sudden panic coming over her.

It couldn't have been the arrival of Hiram at that moment with an amiable stranger in checked suit and Ascot tie who had the mildly annoying habit of twirling a rabbit's foot at the end of his watch chain. In fact, Granny was so unimpressed with Tuck Goodspeed and so annoyed with Hiram that she scarcely acknowledged the introduction.

"Tuck's got something mighty important to tell you, Samantha."

179

"My land, not now," Granny said. "Where's that neat's-foot oil?"

"Lord in heaven," said Hiram. "Where in tarnation did I leave that bottle?"

"This it?" asked the stranger.

"Needs a guardian angel, don't he?" Samantha said testily.

Never one to question a random blessing, she set to work polishing horns and hoofs.

"All animals in the judging ring, please. All animals in the ring at once."

"Guess that'll have to do," Granny said, as Hiram opened the door of the pen.

Now Jeremiah was on his own. In the whole world there was only himself and his lamb walking into that frightening place of judgment. He knew now how the Christian martyrs felt when they went forth into the Roman arena. He needed the aid of someone stronger than himself. He knew he had the love of Granny and Uncle Hiram and Tildy, but it was somehow not enough.

"S'pose he don't win," he whispered to Granny as they parted.

"Happen he don't, I want you to come out of that ring like a Kincaid—walkin' proud."

One foot preceded the other the way they must even on Judgment Day, the lamb followed meekly on his tether. Jerry found himself repeating the opening words of the Twenty-third Psalm, his lips barely moving:

"The Lord is my Shepherd; I shall not want . . ."

He had to hold the leash tightly now, for Danny had found an adversary and playmate in a handsome white snub-nosed Shropshire led by another Pike County boy. The young rams butted playfully, leaped in the air, whirled in the mad excitement of pretended anger.

The three judges, also making their way to the arena, laughed at the mischievous sporting lambs.

"Mighty handsome Shropshire," said one of the judges, "but that black rascal. I wonder . . ."

Their voices were lost in the noise of the crowd,

but Jerry's heart sank in his bosom as he led his lamb along. His beloved Danny was of no breed one could name. Just betwixt and between, a common crossbred sheep of the backwoods variety. What chance did Danny have against these handsome purebred Shropshires, Hampshires, and American Merinos?

"He maketh me to lie down in green pastures:

"He leadeth me beside the still waters.

"He restoreth my soul . . ."

The judging ring was dotted with lambs, each with a handler kneeling beside his entry held on close tether. Jerry kneeled too, his heart beating wildly. Directly behind him along the rail were Granny, Tildy, Uncle Hiram, and the stranger. They would not forsake him in his hour of need. He took some comfort from the appearance of the judges: big men with just but kindly faces; the head judge tall and gravely serious.

As the trio moved from contestant to contestant, the owner's name was called:

"Holloway!" said the leading judge, consulting his clip sheet.

"Johnson County," replied the boy.

"Name of your entry?"

"Holloway's Hampshire. Number six nine two. Out of Midas the Second's Butter Cup Belle, by Crenshaw, Duke of Manchester."

There was a ripple of applause. Jeremiah's heart plummeted. How could Danny hope to match a lamb of such aristocratic lineage?

"Marshall!"

"Pike County."

The applause was deafening. There stood the well-groomed, snub-nosed Shropshire whom the judges had admired when Danny and he were jousting in the areaway. Both owner and ram were obviously popular.

"Name of your entry?"

"Shropshire Lad. Number seven eight seven four. Out of Lassie Queen, by National Grand Champion, Hiram of Troy's Golden Thorn."

Again the burst of applause for the boy and his beautifully fleeced Shropshire. Down the line of young

181

men with their rams came the judges, calling out the names; receiving the proud answers. Jerry looked around him in panic. Yes, there were the only faces he knew in the crowd: Granny with new hat awry, yearning toward him; Tildy with lips slightly apart and cheeks burning with excitement; Hiram chewing nervously on an unlit cigar; and finally the amiable stranger who seemed to radiate confidence.

"Kincaid!"

No answer.

"Kincaid! Come, come, speak up!"

"Pike County," Jeremiah said in a small voice.

"Name of your entry?"

"Dan Patch II."

"What breed, boy? Rambouillet?"

The Twenty-third Psalm was still running through Jeremiah's mind (the words both comforting and gently exacting): "He leadeth me in the paths of righteousness for His Name's sake."

"What breed, son?"

Every eye in the great circle of faces was upon him. "Paths of righteousness." Jerry suddenly knew what the phrase meant. Granny would have to tell them the bitter truth about Danny. He had no right even to let them think he was a Rambouillet or any other pedigreed variety.

"Tell them, Granny," he called to the old woman leaning toward him over the rail.

"You tell them, son. Hold up yore head now!"

Jerry rose from his knees and stood very straight beside his lamb. "This black lamb of mine ain't no fancy purebred," he said in a proud, clear voice. "He's jest a Cat Hollow Kincaid, same as me and Granny."

The crowd was so quiet you could hear the faraway music of the merry-go-round.

"His mam's name was Jezebel. And we ain't quite sure who his pap was."

The crowd burst into raucous laughter.

"Go ahead, laugh," Jeremiah shouted, fighting back the tears. "But he's the best lamb in the world. He ain't afeared of nothin' or nobody. He got lost and he

182

got found again. And he could lick all of these fancy rams any day in the week—like, like David licked Goliath."

The crowd howled with laughter. Men slapped each other on the back and roared. The tall chief judge held up his hand for silence, and said very clearly so that all could hear:

"Nice pair of shoulders on your lamb, my boy. Good quality wool too."

"Yea, though I walk through the Valley of the Shadow of Death I will fear no evil . . ." continued the voice in Jeremiah's mind.

The judges were in conference now, huddled together examining their notebooks. There were no red ribbons nor white ribbons in this particular event. And Jerry knew that in this hard world being second or third meant nothing. His lips were dry and he felt light-headed and a little sick—waiting—waiting.

What could be taking them so long? Time hung suspended like a great hawk over the breathless arena. The sun blazed down on the dusty grass, sending up little heat waves; the pennants drooped in defeat upon the still air. Although Jerry's throat and chest were so constricted he could scarcely breathe, he had a sense of seeing everything with the utmost clarity. Never before had he noticed the fine network of delicate veins in the translucent wings of the dragonfly, nor how its burnished colors change from bronze to purple to peacock blue. Was it good luck that for a moment this gleaming insect (astray from nearby marshes) lit on the tip of Danny's small left horn?

Minutes seemed hours while the judges argued. Jerry felt he could almost read their thoughts as he was trying to read their lips. Surely it was Holloway's Hampshire or Marshall's Shropshire Lad. Both boys were doubtless sons of fathers who were themselves breeders of sheep. They had been born and schooled to raise prize-winning lambs, could choose their entries from great flocks of purebred animals.

And yet a sudden flickering hope sprang up in his heart like the welcome breeze now fluttering the pennants. The Lord God Almighty had fashioned his black lamb; the same Creator who had made the birds of the air and the flowers of the field. What human could improve upon the works of the Almighty? He who with no help of man brought forth each spring the redbud and the mountain laurel, who taught the whippoorwill to sing and the oriole to build its nest.

"God don't need nobody's help," Jeremiah whispered to his lamb. He felt a new fierce pride in Danny's ebony perfection. A Greater Shepherd than Holloway or Marshall had helped Jeremiah raise a winner. A Greater Judge than those three men in conference would confer the prize.

But Jerry's new-found courage faced a bitter test as the judges, nodding solemnly, turned to make the awards. Two steps, three steps—— They were passing him by; they were heading for Holloway—no, they were approaching Marshall. Jeremiah followed with stricken eyes the strides of the tall chief judge as he walked toward the owner of the handsome Shropshire.

There went the coveted blue ribbon. There went the little sack of cash money. The Almighty had forsaken him after all. And yet Jeremiah turned to Him in his agony. "Thy rod and Thy staff, they comfort me . . ."

"The judging committee of the Pike County Agricultural and Livestock Association hereby unanimously confers the blue ribbon and cash award upon Mr. Marshall's Shropshire Lad."

The crowd clapped and shouted. Marshall beamed and shook hands with the judges. Holloway scowled and kicked the dust with his toe. He took his lamb from the line, leading the other contestants from the arena. It seemed to Jeremiah that a cloud had covered the sun. He stood dazed and bewildered as Marshall came past with the blue ribbon proudly attached to his lamb.

"It's all right, Danny," Jerry whispered. "It's all right, boy."

Through unwanted tears Jeremiah saw the blurred figures beyond the rail: Tildy openly weeping, Granny dabbing at her eyes, while Uncle Hiram clamped savage teeth upon the butt of his cigar. But curiously enough the stranger was still smiling with bright, almost angelic calm. He remembered Granny's advice to come out walking proud like a Kincaid, and he straightened his narrow shoulders and began to lead his lamb from the ring. Already the crowd was turning away, unheedful, seeking some new amusement.

"Just a moment, folks," the leading judge shouted. "Wait a minute, young man."

Jeremiah paused uncertainly. "You mean me, sir?"

"I'm talking to you, son."

"I guess we can take our lickin'," Jerry said. "We lost fair and square."

"I like your spirit, boy," the judge said, "and I like your lamb. Only trouble is he's black. Sorta puts him in a class by himself."

The crowd laughed lazily as Jeremiah forced back the tears. He eyed the tall man before him suspiciously, half expecting ridicule; fearing even more any kindly words of consolation.

But the judge raised his hand for silence, and his stern, sincere voice awakened the smallest flame of hope in Jerry's mind.

"Wait, folks. I'm not trying to be funny. This lamb *is* in a class by himself. It happens sometimes that a crossbred lamb is born with almost perfect wool and conformation. Raised on a hill farm with no special breeding behind him, he shows what love and care can do in the production of livestock. He has good lines and a deep, fine fleece. No lamb has ever come into this ring better groomed than Kincaid's Dan Patch II. This young ram is a champion in every sense of the word, therefore . . ."

"Thou preparest a table before me in the presence of mine enemies . . ." said the voice in Jerry's mind.

"Therefore, we wish to confer on Mr. Kincaid and his lamb an award we have not made for the last three years—The Special Award of Merit."

Possibly the crowd was more kindly than Jeremiah had imagined, for they now broke all previous records

185

in their noisy approval as the chief judge took a rosette and ribbon of royal purple silk from a small leather box.

Jeremiah had just reached the line in the Twenty-third Psalm which says very simply, "My cup runneth over."

15 THE HOMECOMING

They had been out and beyond. They had traveled luxuriously on the green-plush seats of Old 99. Now they knew what lay beyond the far bend in the tracks, what the Main Street of Midlothian looked like, and how it felt to ride on the Ferris wheel and the merry-go-round. They had won ribbons and held up their heads among outlanders.

More than all this they had learned from an eyewitness facts which were subtly to alter all of their lives. Tuck Goodspeed seemed providentially sent to tell the final chapter in the lives of Seth and Arabella. Jeremiah's great-grandfather Henderson (father of Lilith and grandfather of Arabella) had employed one of the finest trainers in the bluegrass to manage his stable and his affairs.

Goodspeed had managed the horses well and the affairs badly. Nothing was left of the modest fortune, all of which had disappeared before the old man's death. But Tuck could tell them that Jeremiah's parents were not quite as Granny had always pictured them. And Granny was in a mood to accept Tuck's revelations.

"You mean that traipsin' fiddlin' woman done right by my Seth?"

"Well," said Tuck, "she did go to live with her grandpap Henderson one winter while Seth took a job in Chicago."

"How about the way she killed him apurpose in that burning stable?"

"Ma'am, you got that story all mixed up," Tuck said in amiable rebuttal. "Sure they nipped each other now and then like any high-strung thoroughbreds. But they was as loving a pair as you could ask, the night of the fire. Seth was back from Chicago. We all was sound asleep when we heard the crackle and roar of the flames and the screams of the horses. You can't never forget a stable fire. I still wake up in a cold sweat dreaming about it."

"Sent him in to save her horse; sent Seth in to his death," Granny insisted.

"Didn't do no such thing, ma'am. Seth was bound and determined to save that filly on account of the way Arabella loved the little mare. Broke away from his wife, Seth did, and plunged into that roaring fire. Then Arabella went right in after him."

"You tellin' me the Gospel truth, Tuck Goodspeed?"

"Swear it on a stack of Bibles."

"Wal," said Samantha, "it jest goes to show. Cain't never tell about true love. Guess I'll have to change the last few verses of my song ballad. Burned to a crisp in each other's arms, no doubt. It's a real sad story."

Now steaming up the track on the way back to their cabin they were tired but deeply contented, hungry with longing for Fulton Corners and Cat Hollow, their own streams and meadows, their own pocket in the hills. They wanted to hear once again the fiddle music from the violin that Tuck Goodspeed had shipped to Tarleton's Mill on Bean Blossom Creek. They needed the sound of remembered voices.

Now they were rounding the curve that for so many years had been the farthest horizon of their lives; they were listening to the hollow thunder of the train crossing the trestle. Jeremiah's heart missed a beat, for there was the grain elevator and the water tank, and the little church and Grundy's store, the grandest sight in this or any other world.

"Granny, Tildy, Uncle Hiram! We're home."

"Land of Goshen," said Granny as Highball Johnson pulled up at the station. "What's all the ruckus?"

They didn't know that Uncle Hiram had squandered thirty-five cents to wire the good news to Pete Grundy.

"A band and everything," Tildy cried. "Look, there's my mam waving like crazy."

"Hmmm," said Hiram. "A committee of welcome."

It was just the way Jeremiah always wanted to remember it. Fud Grundy shouting, "She's ablowin' for a stop." Folks pouring out of every door; hound-dogs ambling sleepily toward the station; colts high-tailing through the pastures.

"Sounds like an infare at a crazy house," Granny said happily, as tin pans, banjoes, harmonicas, and fiddles took up the welcome.

Willing hands helped Bob Peters lift down Danny's crate and the box of covers. "Stand back, folks. Don't want to scare this prize lamb."

"Well, what do you know!" "The special award." "Allus did say that boy and lamb would make their mark in this world." "Kin I touch him, Jerry?"

"How'd you like ridin' on the cars, Granny?"

"It's better'n walkin'," Granny said.

"Quiet, folks! Quiet, please," said Pete Grundy. "When it comes to takin' ribbons, there ain't no flies on Fulton Corners."

Cheers!

"Now this here's my party," Grundy shouted; "got two cases of lemon soda on ice; got six watermelons and a big freezer full of chocolate ice cream."

More cheers.

"Line up," roared Pete Grundy, "two double abreast

like a real parade. I'm furnishing the eats free for nothing."

"But what'll I do with Danny?" Jerry asked.

"Why, bring him along. Bring him in the store," said Pete Grundy. "It's his party."

Hours later, driving out to Cat Hollow in Uncle Hiram's jolt wagon, the old horse suddenly reared as Lafe Tarleton stepped through a gap in the hedge. If Samantha had been able to reach the whip she would have larruped either the horse or Lafe. But Hiram shouted "Whoa," and pulled to a stop.

"Howdy, Lafe!"

The man could only answer with his eyes, which did not seem evil or angry. From beneath his arm he took a large parcel wrapped in brown paper. He handed it humbly to Jeremiah, who knew instinctively it was his mam's fiddle, the violin they so often heard on summer nights far up the hollow.

"I cain't take it, Uncle Lafe," Jeremiah said.

"Take it, son. Lafe wants you to have it," Uncle Hiram advised; "you're next of kin, boy. Someday Lafe'll be leaving you his house and mill and lands."

Lafe Tarleton nodded his head in happy agreement. He helped unwrap the fiddle, then motioned for Jeremiah to tuck it under his chin and try the fiddle bow.

"Oh, thank you kindly," Jeremiah said; "it's what I've always craved to remember my mam by."

A moment later Lafe had disappeared as quietly as he had come, and they were jogging along once again toward the cabin in Cat Hollow. There was a whole world of joy ahead. Jeremiah would take fiddle lessons from Lafe himself. He would try to catch the Big One, lying sulkily in the deep hole beneath the bridge. He would always have his lamb and Tildy and Granny and Uncle Hiram. Next year he would be in fifth grade.

"That was real neighborly of Lafe," Granny said, sighing happily.

"Satisfied, Samantha?" Hiram asked.

"I'm that satisfied," said Samantha Kincaid, "I don't reckon I'll budge ten steps out of Cat Hollow the rest

190

of my born days. I aim to take a settin' chair out under the trumpet vines, and set there listenin' to Jeremiah play the fiddle, arestin' my bones till Judgment Day. Satisfied? I'm so satisfied I'm plumb miserable."